HEARTS ON HER SHADOWS

DIXIE LYNN DWYER

MENAGE EVERLASTING

Siren Publishing, Inc.
www.SirenPublishing.com

A SIREN PUBLISHING BOOK
IMPRINT: Ménage Everlasting

HEARTS ON FIRE 9: HER SHADOWS OF LIGHT
Copyright © 2016 by Dixie Lynn Dwyer

ISBN: 978-1-68295-788-2

First Printing: November 2016

Cover design by Les Byerley
All art and logo copyright © 2016 by Siren Publishing, Inc.

Printed in the U.S.A.

PUBLISHER
Siren Publishing, Inc.
www.SirenPublishing.com

DEDICATION

Dear readers,

Thank you for purchasing this legal copy of *Her Shadows of Light*.

Brighid is a strong, independent woman, but following her gut instincts takes practice and a new mindset to trust in. Learning to follow her gut, to be honest with her emotions can either make or break the relationship with the four new men in her life.

May you enjoy Brighid's story as she does things the hard way and risks just about everything to ensure her lovers are safe, and they can move on with life together.

Happy Reading,

Hugs!

~Dixie~

HEARTS ON FIRE 9: HER SHADOWS OF LIGHT

DIXIE LYNN DWYER
Copyright © 2016

Prologue

"We call you when we need your services. You don't call us and demand more work. You don't like it, then tough. We need to make this move and slow down so more red flags don't pop up," Lenny told him over the phone.

"Those red flags aren't my fault. They're yours," Stark replied.

"Mine? I don't think so, guy. No one was supposed to get killed. The old lady was supposed to live. You fucked up, and we need to make some changes. Now don't call me again. I'll call you when I need another job done," Lenny said to him and then hung up.

Stark was pissed off. When he'd first started working for Lenny, things had been different. They knew to never ask his name or to meet in person. Once he performed a few small jobs for them, they'd started giving him bigger ones. It was all good, and it helped him deal with his anger, his obsession.

He clenched his teeth. Why did Lucie have to be such a nag? Why had she walked in on him talking about that next job? Why had she been nagging him about getting engaged and getting married? That wasn't what he wanted. Years ago he'd thought that was what his future would entail, but given the circumstances of his childhood and the evaluations the doctors had come up with, it seemed he wasn't normal.

It hadn't taken much to silence Lucie's threats of going to the police and reporting him as an arsonist. Killing her so easily made him feel powerful, whole, and on the top of his game. He'd stared at the flame as he lit the match, holding it against the wall as the sunlight penetrated through the window. It didn't cause a shadow of the flame to appear.

He found that to be so interesting. He'd inhaled the scent of burning wood and tossed the match into the fire he'd started. His mind no longer obsessed over his loss or over the several other women who had become his symbols. They were gone. Dead. Worthless to anyone now, especially to him. They'd served their purpose by serving him, by lying on the table, begging for mercy, and ultimately begging for death.

That somber, gut-wrenching emotion of killing Lucie and the other women, women he believed could be his hold on sanity, had now been replaced by something even greater. It was the adrenaline rush, the soulful, magical power of fire. The need for his talent, his capability, brought him things he'd never thought he would ever be able to have. Money, meaning, power, and all because of the ability to make fire that destroyed. Fire that annihilated everything, every ounce of evidence, every possible culprit or fingerprint, footstep, creation that he made in order to succeed. He was a fire starter, a paid arsonist, for lack of a more suitable title. He wasn't a loser, a psychologically imbalanced threat to society as the doctors all tried to label him. No. He was more than they gave him credit for, and that was why they all suffered, too. But he didn't mind those memories and hurtful reminders of the past anymore because the trick was on them, not him.

The others, the ones seeking to manipulate the system and get filthy rich by breaking the law, bought into his practice, his capabilities, and they made money, too. He wanted more. He desired more, and them moving their business wouldn't stop him. He sought something with even greater meaning and feelings of accomplishment. He took every job Lenny and Ray gave to him because he was searching for that missing aspect. Even setting this latest fire and causing the death of the older woman could have been avoided, but he was seeking that urge, that itch. Her dying didn't do a thing for his needs and desires. In fact, it made him think about what could replace that empty gap or fill it. How would he know what it was? What if he missed it?

He rocked back and forth in his chair and reached out to press the key on the laptop. He loved reading inspirational quotes, even sayings from the Bible that he felt reflected what was in his mind or his agenda. Today was no different, just that the urge for more was beginning to really eat at his insides.

The words appeared on the computer screen. His power, his direction, his motivation. He wasn't a monster. He wasn't evil per se. He was highly motivated to feel, to succeed in being one with the light and no longer a shadow, a mere presence taking up space. He wanted to feel renewed, alive, all powerful, and have meaning.

He continued to rock back and forth as he scanned the words and felt their energy, their meaning to his heart.

"The Bible says, 'God is Light, in him there is no darkness at all.' 1 John 1:5.

"I am a prophet of God, and fire is my weapon to lay down an assault on those who stand in the way of my greatness. I shall battle through the fires of hell to find what is missing and what is mine. It's out there. I just need to keep the light burning bright so that it can find me or I can find it."

Chapter 1

Brighid Murphy was laughing along with her friends Jenny and Anna as they stood by the crowded bar. It was nearly eleven when a group of strapping, sexy guys entered the bar lounge. At least ten invaded the place, catching the attention of not only her and her other friends but also that of every female with clear enough vision to see they were eye candy and a half. She actually felt her body react to the good-looking men.

"Holy shit, look at that guy's ass in those jeans and all those muscles on his arms. Someone get me some ice. I feel a hot flash coming over me big time." Anna waved her hand in front of her face, fanning herself.

"I'll take three of those and maybe a fourth. I'm feeling extra special tonight," Jenny said to the bartender, who chuckled and then set out three shots of tequila for them.

"Oh no, I don't think I should. I have work Monday, and I'll need more then Saturday and Sunday to recover." Brighid glanced at the men who'd walked in and were now moving closer toward the bar and all the ladies hanging around it.

The bachelorette party had been sort of lame, especially since the bride-to-be only lasted an hour and got so drunk she had to be carried to her room. At least the party still continued, and it was the maid of honor who had to babysit, not them. Brighid wasn't even friends with the woman. Jenny was, but Jenny hated most of the crowd so she'd dragged Brighid and Anna along to enjoy the night.

"Good evening, ladies, could we squeeze in here to grab a few beers?" one deep, sexy voice said over Brighid's shoulder. As she turned to look up, way up, she locked gazes with one hell of a sexy man. He had dark hair and big brown eyes, and he seemed really intrigued by her lips, if how he stared at them was any indication.

"Sure thing, doll. You can sit on my lap if you need a spot." Jenny winked.

He chuckled, and so did his buddy, who eased right next to Brighid on her other side, moving her friends out of the way. But Jenny and Anna didn't seem to care, as a few other men joined them and began conversing.

"Two Heinekens please," one guy asked the bartender. Then he looked back at her.

"What's your name?" he asked.

"Brighid."

"I'm Rusty, and this is my brother, Reece."

He stuck out his hand for her to shake. She reached out, and when their hands touched, his eyes widened and she felt something, a low, trembling hum of awareness, an instant attraction. She pulled her hand back, and his brother smiled as he checked her out. He reached his hand out, held her gaze, and gave her the once-over as she shook his hand.

"You live around here?" Reece asked her.

She was mesmerized by Reece's dark blue eyes and both the very intricate, black tattoo on his arm and the other colorful one on the inside of his wrist.

"No, just attending a bachelorette party with some friends."

"Not yours, I hope," Rusty teased and winked then passed the beer bottle to his brother before taking a sip from his own.

She felt her cheeks warm. He was pretty flirty. "Not me. I actually don't even know the bride to be. My friends dragged me along. How about you? Do you two brothers live around here?"

For some reason, as she looked from one brother to the other, she imagined what it would be like to be squeezed between them, with both men touching her at once. A ménage encounter was something she'd fantasized about, but it was more out of the desire to have a man or men that would really care about her and not just want to fuck her because of her body. She worked out a lot, and she had a sexy figure. Getting dates wasn't the problem. It was accepting them, needing more than just a sexual encounter. She'd had three separate lovers over the years, and none of them had really done it for her. The need for more, to feel a depth she'd only read about, ruled her mind and her decision to stop dating for a while.

Why was she thinking about this right now and with these two brothers?

She knew why, because her friends had been hounding her to have a great time tonight, to forget about the past and the fact that she was transferring to a new job location with the company she worked for. It hadn't been what she expected, but her bosses, Lenny and Ray, said it was necessary. They offered her a great salary, full benefits, and flexible hours. Tonight was a last hurrah to let go and embrace the future and the professional career she had worked hard for.

"We came out to visit some friends of ours. One of our buddies is getting married in a few months, but this is a pre-bachelor party," Reece told her.

"A pre-bachelor party? Never heard of such a thing."

She smiled as his brother Rusty moved closer to her. His body was lightly brushing against hers, and she couldn't ignore the sexual energy vibrating between the three of them. Add in that cologne he was wearing and she was feeling aroused and attracted to both men. What the heck was going on?

Rusty chuckled. "It was an excuse to come party and have some fun. We're busy working all the time, so this weekend forced us to let loose a little."

"Sounds like you have demanding jobs. What do you two do for a living?"

Reece smirked. "We're firefighters, ma'am," he said in a sexy, flirty tone that made her belly quiver. The nervousness made her chuckle.

"Hey, hey, shots all around. Let's do this!" one of their friends yelled, and Brighid looked at them and Jenny and Anna, who were practically hanging on the arms of the two guys.

"I don't think so," Brighid said, thinking someone would have to help her friends get to the room.

"Oh no you don't. It's your weekend to let loose too, Miss Prim and Proper. Shots all around," Jenny said, and the bartender lined them up.

"Here you go, Miss Prim and Proper." Rusty winked then began passing her one. She shook her head and smirked but took the shot glass. He and his brother took one too, and then the others counted to three and they all did the shots then cheered.

"You didn't even make a strange face. You like tequila?" Reece asked her as he placed his hand on the back of her chair.

"I don't dislike it. I'm really not a shot kind of person, but it has been a hell of a few weeks with work."

Then the bartender poured another round.

By the fourth shot, she was starting to loosen up and so were Rusty and Reece.

"Where do you work?" Reece asked, and she felt his hand begin to play with her hair as Rusty sat down on the bar stool next to her and placed his hand over her knee.

"You've got gorgeous green eyes, sweetie. I don't think I've ever seen such beautiful eyes."

His voice and their simultaneous touch were playing havoc on her body and her brain. She knew she shouldn't tell them too much about herself, but they were so damn nice.

"I work for an insurance firm. I'm heading out to New Orleans Monday morning for a new position." She lied. She was heading an hour away to New Jersey and a town called Treasure Town, which was supposed to be awesome. Her bosses at the insurance firm had even hooked her up with a condo there near the beach. She had her bikinis all picked out and hoped to get a bit of sun in during the weekends.

"Insurance, huh? That's great. I've been to New Orleans a few times. Where will you be working?" Rusty asked and then took another slug of beer.

She started talking about Louisiana, which she did know a bit about, having cousins out there. In fact, she had a few who were firefighters and police officers.

"You have cousins in that area who work as cops and firefighters? Damn, I knew I liked you." Reece moved his hand under her hair and gave her neck a gentle squeeze.

It sure did affect her in ways she wasn't used to. They were absolutely perfect, but this situation and meeting here wasn't.

They were more than likely out for a good time. Well, she was too, but she didn't sleep around, although these two would be a fantasy come true. Still, she wasn't stupid.

As they continued to talk, she found out they had a lot in common and were both New York Giants fans. That got them talking about sports, which she knew a lot more about than most women did.

"Another round, on us this time," one of their friends called out, and they handed out shots again.

A little while later, they walked toward the pool table set up in the bar area and started playing a few games while her friends made out with the two guys they'd just met.

Time seemed to go by so quickly, and she really was having a fun time with Reece and Rusty. She knew she shouldn't keep drinking, but they were all enjoying themselves, and she was loosening up so much she started touching Reece and Rusty, running her hands along their muscles.

At one point she was asking about Rusty's tattoo on his wrist and noticed a cut along his arm.

He pulled her onto his lap on one of the small couches in the pool area and told her how he'd sustained the injury during a fire just yesterday.

She was impressed but also turned on by him and his brother who sat on the arm of the chair and caressed her hair. She didn't think twice when she brought Rusty's wrist to her lips and kissed the cut.

His eyes darkened, and he looked at her then her lips right before he pulled her close and kissed her.

That kiss grew deeper until he released her lips and exhaled.

"Holy shit, Brighid."

She felt exactly the same way. Never had she felt so in tune to a man. Well, to two men at once, as Reece touched her chin and tilted it up toward him. She stared up into his dark blue eyes.

"I want to taste you, too."

She pulled her bottom lip between her teeth and wondered if she should or not.

Then Rusty caressed her hair and ran his hand along her leg and her knee.

"Go on and kiss my brother. We share everything, and you're too perfect for us not to let him kiss you, too."

She swallowed hard and noticed her friends were having a great time, as were the men's friends. So when Reece leaned down and pressed his lips to hers, she was shocked when she felt just as connected and attracted to Reece as she did when she'd kissed Rusty.

"Jesus, Brighid. You taste so sweet."

He gave her a wink, and she smiled and then looked at her friends.

This was what tonight was all about. Having a good time, letting loose, meeting new people, and not having any regrets. But as more shots were passed around and she started to feel numb and as if she never wanted this night to end, she let go and decided to live for once in her life instead of being a stickler for rules and order. There was plenty of time for that when she started her new job.

* * * *

Rusty couldn't believe their luck. Brighid was gorgeous, sexy, classy, and so much fun he didn't want the night to end. He was pissed off that she was moving to Louisiana. He tried to figure out a way to see her again, maybe visit her. She was that fucking perfect. Reece was holding her hand and walking with her out of the lounge area and toward the hallway. They were all feeling pretty damn drunk. Her friends had taken off with some of their friends an hour ago, but she didn't seem like the kind of woman who slept around. It was three o'clock in the morning, and the bar was clearing out. He wondered if they could make plans for tomorrow.

As he stood up to follow them out of the room, he felt the room spinning and so did Reece.

"Holy shit, I think you got me drunk, Brighid," Reece said to her, and she wrapped her arm around his waist and chuckled.

"Don't worry, fireman Reece. I've got you."

Reece chuckled and ran his hand along her ass. He gave it a slap, and she gasped and then laughed. "I think I like being got."

Rusty took position on her other side and grabbed onto her waist.

"I think you got us both drunk." Rusty tried to focus on where they were headed.

"I've got you too, so no worries, sir." She saluted and nearly fell forward.

Rusty didn't know how he caught her, but thank God, his reflexes weren't totally off, or she would have fallen on her face. It was bad enough her heels were making her wobble.

"Wait. Hold up." Reece slid from her hold, went down on one knee, teetered a moment, and looked up into her eyes. Rusty, despite seeing two of Reece, could see the desire and attraction in his brother's eyes.

"Give me these heels, baby, before you break your pretty little neck."

"Aw, that's so sweet, Reece." She leaned forward to hold on to his shoulders and then hugged him, her breasts against his face.

Reece lifted her up and kissed her. Rusty joined in, feeling her body beneath his palms as he rubbed them along her hips and then her shoulders. He kissed her neck and suckled her skin. God, he wanted her so badly his cock ached with need.

"Get a fucking room," someone yelled, and Rusty turned to see some guy with his woman.

Reece laughed after he released her lips.

"I think he's right." Reece took her hand and led them to the elevator.

* * * *

Reece pressed Brighid against the wall in the elevator. He moved his hands along her hips and then cupped her breasts, shocked at how full and large she felt. He'd never been so attracted to a woman before, and this one had to be leaving for another job out of state. It sucked. He didn't want to let her go, and surely didn't want the night to end, but how could they make her stay with them?

She kissed him back and then slowly moved her lips to the side to breathe.

"God, you two are such good kissers. I don't want this night to end."

He smiled. "We don't either."

She smiled, and then he leaned his forehead against hers and felt the hallway spinning.

"Jesus, I'm fucking drunk as hell."

"Me, too. I feel numb."

Then the door to the room opened, and Reece saw Rusty wobble and hit the door. Brighid chuckled and then wrapped her arm around Reece's waist and walked with him into the room.

That was when things got crazy. He and Rusty stared at her, both of them rocking on their feet.

"I know this is crazy, and you don't know us, but I want you so badly."

He reached for her, almost missing her waist, and he gripped her hips and pressed her backward. She held on as he swooped down to kiss her lips before they landed on the bed.

He pulled back. "Oh God, I should go. I'm so tipsy."

She cupped his cheek. "But you're gorgeous and sweet."

The bed dipped, and Rusty plopped down beside them.

"And what about me?" he asked with a silly grin.

She chuckled and then looked so serious. She cupped his chin.

"You're gorgeous, too."

She kissed him, and then Reece began to undress her, spreading kisses along her skin and her breasts. The room continued to move, but all he cared about was spending more time with Brighid and waking up with her in between them in the morning.

* * * *

Brighid woke up feeling as though she was in a cocoon of warmth. Her mouth felt so dry, her head was aching, and she could barely open her eyes.

As she blinked them open, she saw a man, a very large, muscular, naked man lying in front of her. She moved and heard a moan then felt a hand land on her hip and pull her back against him.

Not one man. Two men were in bed with her, and they were all naked. She felt his hard thighs and then saw that the hand on her hip had a tattoo on its wrist.

Oh shit. The firefighters from last night. Oh God, I slept with two men, brothers.

As her mind processed what had happened, she began to panic. She slowly eased her way out of their holds and they both moaned and moved onto their backs.

She somehow, still feeling tipsy, maneuvered out from between them. She stepped between Rusty's thighs and then onto the floor, losing her balance and falling and then praying she didn't wake them. She gripped the edge of the bed and stared at them. *Don't wake up. Oh God, please don't wake up.*

She looked for her dress and her panties. Finding them, she bent to get into them. Her whole body ached, and her breasts were full and aroused.

I get so drunk I fuck two men and fulfill a fantasy and I don't remember any bit of it? Oh God, what the hell did I do? She stared at their bodies. She would love to take a picture. Hell, she would put it up in her bedroom and masturbate over them every night. They were that fucking sexy. *What the hell am I thinking? I can't believe I just thought that. That is so not me. Freaking tequila. It screwed up my brain. Oh God, I'm a slut. Jesus…no, not Jesus, don't bring up his name. Oh God, I am never going to tell a soul about this.*

She grabbed her bag and her heels and took one last look at the two sexiest, amazing men she had ever met. If circumstances were different, and she weren't leaving, or maybe had time to date them before she slept with them, there could be a chance. They were so perfect, she would have thought they'd been made for her and her for them. They were so in tune to one another, and there was that connection. Well, obviously a big connection.

She bit her lip. Tears filled her eyes. She was such an idiot. *And I can't remember any of it. I hope it was incredible. I hope I was incredible. Fuck.*

She hurried toward the door and then slowly, and as quietly as possible, exited the room.

No one would ever know this secret. She wouldn't tell a soul. She stood out in the hallway and took a few unsteady breaths.

She laid her head against the wall, needing a moment to stop the walls from looking as if they were moving. God, I'm still drunk. She smiled to herself as little bits of memory invaded her mind and her body buzzed with awareness. *That was the best night of my life. I'll never forget Rusty and Reece. Keep them safe in their jobs, and please make sure I never see them again or I'll be mortified.*

Her phone started ringing in her bag, surprising her, and she hurried away from the door and to the stairwell. She answered the phone.

"Brighid, I need a ride. Don't ask me any questions. I drank way too much last night, and I just woke up in bed with a man I think I met last night."

Brighid smiled. "Don't worry, Jenny. Your secret's safe with me."

Chapter 2

"What the fuck is your problem, Rusty?" his brother Pat asked as they unloaded the trunk from food shopping. It was Sunday, and they were all off from work.

"Nothing," he mumbled.

"That must have been some fucking weekend to keep you in this shit-ass mood," Pat replied.

"Leave him alone," Reece chimed in.

Pat raised his hands up in surrender, and then he grabbed another two bags and chuckled as he headed into the house.

"What's the yelling all about?" his brother Tobin, the oldest and a detective in a special investigative unit in Treasure Town, asked.

He was logging the receipt from the store into the computer. They budgeted out everything and tried to keep track of their spending habits. Not that they had to, but that was just how organized Tobin was. He was a true disciplinary and expected respect at all levels and in all relationships and connections. Sometimes he was too hard, but Pat wouldn't dare start that fight up with him.

"They're both in rotten moods still?" Tobin asked as he closed up the laptop and went back to unpacking the groceries.

"Yeah, it must have been a shitty fucking weekend. I'm glad we were tied up with work. They didn't even say if Ron had a good time at his pre-bachelor party," Pat said.

"He had a great time. He's already planning the real bachelor party and expects you two to be there," Reece told them as he placed the last few bags onto the kitchen table. Rusty brought in the beer. He placed it into the refrigerator and then helped out with the other items.

Rusty slammed the cabinet door, and Reece dropped a box of pasta then put it into the cupboard before slamming that door next. Pat looked at Tobin, who appeared to be getting tired of their bad fucking moods as he stared at them.

"Okay, enough is enough. What the fuck happened over the weekend at that party that has you two moping around, slamming cabinets, and being dicks to everyone?" Tobin crossed his arms in front of his chest and gave them that stern interrogation expression that worked on thugs. It didn't quite work on them, but they were brothers. They shared just about everything, so why weren't Reece and Rusty sharing this?

"We're not moping around or being dicks. We're just tired from the weekend," Reece added, and Rusty plopped down in the chair, popped open a beer, and guzzled half its contents down.

Tobin looked at Rusty, and Pat knew something big was up, but before he could ask, Tobin took the lead.

"Shit, what the fuck happened? Spill the beans now," Tobin demanded in that tone of his. "We're brothers, and we don't keep secrets."

Pat watched Rusty and Reece exchange looks.

"Hand me a beer. If we're going to tell them what happened, I'll need a few of those."

Rusty reached back, opened the refrigerator door, grabbed three more beers, and placed them onto the table then closed the door.

Reece pushed two across the table for Tobin and Pat.

They popped them open, the sound filtering through the room, adding to the connection, the equality and bond they had.

Reece looked at Rusty. "We met a woman."

Pat put the beer down and looked at Tobin, who squinted when he looked at his brothers.

"She was fucking amazing. Beautiful, both outside and inside. A knockout," Reece stated.

"We all got drunk. She's from out of town, leaving for a new job tomorrow morning in Louisiana. She was attending a bachelorette party with friends, and, well, we hit it off. We had so much shit in common. The chemistry was fucking incredible," Rusty said, and Reece nodded.

"So what happened?" Tobin asked.

"We woke up the next morning, and she was fucking gone." Rusty clenched his teeth, and the vein at his temple was pulsating.

His brother was really upset about this.

"So you two fuck some hot chick and she sneaks out in the morning and you're acting like this? Why? Obviously it didn't mean shit to her. She doesn't even live nearby. It was a fucking one-night stand." Tobin took a slug from his beer.

"No, it was incredible. I mean, like lightning striking. My fucking dick was never so hard just from looking at a woman, never mind talking to her," Rusty said.

"She was sweet, Tobin. I think she panicked because she got drunk too, and the three of us didn't want the night to end. It was like nothing I've ever felt before. Every little touch affected Rusty and me. It was instant, and everything about her was perfect from her long red hair, big green eyes, and exceptional figure to her personality. I can't stop thinking about her and what could have been," Reece admitted.

Tobin ran his fingers through his hair. "Jesus, you two are fucking serious?" Tobin sat down at the kitchen table.

"Dead serious." Reece drank down the rest of the beer in the can. Rusty opened up the refrigerator and pulled out four more beers.

"Did you try asking at the hotel to find out who she was, her name and number, anything?" Pat asked.

"Dude, do we looking fucking stupid?" Rusty said. "Once we got over the fact that she'd snuck out, figuring she was probably embarrassed because she didn't seem like a woman who did shit like that all the time, we went down to the front desk and asked. They wouldn't tell us shit. Thought we were some stalkers or something."

"That's hotel policy. They can't disclose information on people to strangers. How about her friends or other members of the bachelorette party?" Pat asked.

"We put in calls to some of the guys. We know two were hitting on her girlfriends, so we're hoping to find something out that way," Reece said.

"Well, I hate to say it, but there isn't much you can do about it. Even if you did find out her full name, her number and address, you aren't going to fly out to another state just to talk to her and see where it will lead. Leave it as a memory of an unforgettable night. There isn't much more to do." Tobin opened the other beer, took a sip, then stood up and continued to put the stuff away.

"It sucks. She was gorgeous, sexy as damn hell, with a knock-out body," Rusty told them.

"She even had a tattoo on her hip and one on the inside of her wrist. They were both small dragonflies," Reece told Pat.

"Those are distinguishing marks. Maybe you'll hear from one of the guys, and it will lead to her number. If that happens, I would call her first before showing up on her doorstep. Then she'll call the cops on you guys, especially if she only slept with you because she was drunk."

"Fuck you, that wasn't the only reason," Reece said and threw one of the bags at Pat's head.

"The attraction was instant. There was a connection there, and that's what I don't understand," Rusty said.

"Let's say this hot, sexy woman felt it, too. Maybe she figured it wasn't worth it to continue something that would end up nowhere. She isn't even in this state. She's nowhere near here. Just put her out of your heads. It wasn't meant to be," Tobin stated firmly, and it was obvious to Pat that the conversation was over as far as Tobin was concerned.

"I don't know. It was special. I never felt like that before." Rusty played with the rim of his beer can.

"Me either. Who knows? If it's meant to be, we'll meet her again. If not, then every woman we meet from here on out will be compared to her," Reece said, and Rusty agreed.

Pat looked at his brothers. He not only felt bad for them. He also felt envious. This woman really had made an impression. The effect she had on them made him want to meet her, too. But obviously that just wasn't going to happen. They had yet to find a woman the four of them liked in that way. Considering the current circumstances, it wasn't looking as though this particular woman was going to break their streak of no luck.

* * * *

"I don't have time to talk. I just got into the office and it's crazy busy already. I'll call you later, Jenny."

"You'd better," Jenny said, and then Brighid disconnected the call.

She punched the information into the computer and worked diligently to get things started. Her bosses, Lenny McCoy and Ray Syrias, were in Lenny's office with the door closed. Something was going on.

She took a deep breath and thought about why Jenny was calling her this morning of all mornings. For a woman who wanted to forget about a one-night stand with some amazing firefighter, she sure wouldn't stop talking about the guy or his friends. Hence why Brighid didn't want to discuss it. She was so embarrassed for sleeping with two brothers she didn't know and for not even remembering most of it. Throughout Sunday, she kept remembering little things. The feel of their bodies, the touch of their hands, and the way they'd undressed her and explored her together.

She was glad she was on birth control and had an IUD, or she would be worrying now about pregnancy. By mid-week that worry would change to possible contracting some sexually transmitted disease from them. They were so hot. They could have their choice of women. In fact, women probably lined up to get fucked by them.

She banged a little too hard on the keyboard, and it lifted up and banged back down. Why did the thought of them being with other women upset her so much and make her feel jealous? She was never going to see them again. So it didn't matter that she really liked them and that they were perfect for her and they'd had so much in common. It wasn't meant to be. *Now get back to work and focus on making money to pay for the condo and living expenses.* She didn't want to hit up her savings at all.

"Brighid, do you have the file from the Anders investigation handy, or is it still in the boxes? We tried so hard to get everything set over the weekend but it's been nuts. Especially hiring a few more office assistants," Lenny asked her.

"I think I just set that one into the filing cabinet. I already downloaded the documents, scanned them, and saved them on the portable hard drive."

"Great. Can you send that over to me please?"

"Is everything okay with that case? It has been closed for a few weeks."

"Yeah, there was just something we needed to look over. There's a number we need from one of the contacts in there."

She stood up. "I can check it out for you. What's the name and number?" she asked, taking her pen and pad and looking at him.

"That won't be necessary. You continue getting everything into the system. We expect some new clients this week and want you to be on top of the organization to ensure no mistakes are made."

"Okay." Her gut clenched. It was awfully weird for him to react to her like that. Over the past two years, they always had her look things like that up. Unless they had some sort of personal attachment to the case, which was rare.

She went back to work, trying to remain focused on the job and not on the two firefighters who'd changed her life from just one night.

* * * *

"What are we going to do? We're not here in this town for two days and this guy won't leave us alone," Lenny stated.

"Fuck him. He isn't going to do shit, Lenny. We've covered our tracks. We're in charge. It doesn't matter what he wants. He's the best guy out there, and he's all ours."

Lenny ran his fingers through his hair.

"He's been acting funny for several months now. What if he screws up a deal and we get caught? We'll lose everything."

"It's not going to happen. We got away with the last fire where the old lady was killed. We'll continue to get away with this. Don't go gaining some sort of conscience now. He gets paid too good, and he likes doing this shit. Maybe he wants more money, a bigger piece of the action? I don't know. If you're worried, we'll lay low for a while. We'll tell him we don't have any jobs for him right now. Maybe he'll hook up with someone else. He did some work for Baragio."

"Baragio hasn't shown his face for months. Not after that criminal investigation by the feds."

"Which is another reason to not piss the guy off. Listen, it's all good. We'll be fine," Ray stated with a confidence that Lenny just didn't feel.

"No one expects anything. We help law enforcement officers, firefighters, and military people, too. In a town like this, no one will expect shit. Believe me, we'll be back on track, rolling in the dough, and our little friend will be the happy little arsonist he enjoys being. I have a few possible new cases lined up. I'll be meeting the clients and seeing where things are. It will all work out."

"I sure hope you're right about this, Ray, because right now, I'm not feeling too certain at all."

* * * *

The first few weeks of work had passed quickly. They were incredibly busy and had a series of insurance claims concerning fires in the business district a few towns over. She had taken a call for Lenny from some irate customer who claimed that he should have gotten a bigger payout than what he had gotten. It happened often and was based on the plan people had and how much they contributed to that insurance and what it covered. This particular man was seriously misguided and demanding to speak with Lenny. She connected the call and heard Lenny raising his voice. When he came out after the call, he advised her to not patch through any of the calls to him again.

She'd noticed a change in Lenny and Ray recently. They were on edge and not really talking with the three other new staff members in the office. She had taken on the role of office manager, and they seemed fine with that. She kept abreast of what was going on and tried handling situations she knew how to handle and then called in Lenny or Ray to handle the things she wasn't certain of or felt responsible for.

The business was expanding. They were picking up accounts across the United States, and with the expansion, more incidents popped up. Plus, Lenny was taking a key interest in certain cases, never even letting her see the files or assist even with correspondence. It was kind of upsetting. That, of course, made her suspicious of their behavior. Could they be up to something illegal? If so, she wouldn't want to be attached to it. That made her think about how much trouble she could get into. She needed this job. She didn't have any family and didn't know any people other than her bosses and staff members, who were new to the area, too. It made her feel uneasy, but then she convinced herself that she was jumping the gun and drawing conclusions that probably weren't true.

The front door to the main office opened, and a man stepped inside. Normally the front desk secretary handled any walk-ins, but

Lisa had just walked away from her desk to grab a coffee and use the ladies room.

Gina helped him. "Hello, how may I help you?"

"Looking to see Lenny and Ray." He scanned the area. He was an attractive man. Tall, like six feet three, and dressed nicely. He wore designer dress pants, a black belt with silver clip, and a dark green button-down shirt. Then his eyes locked onto hers.

She immediately looked away from him. There was something in his eyes that unnerved her. She swallowed hard.

"They're in a meeting right now. Is there anything I can assist you with? Are you a client?" Gina asked.

The man ignored her and started walking farther into the office.

"They'll see me."

Brighid could see that the man was getting angry. Her bosses were in a meeting with some clients and had asked not to be disturbed. Now Gina was appearing frazzled, and considering Brighid was the main office admin, she decided the help out.

She stood up from her desk and smoothed her hands down her Ann Taylor navy blue dress.

"Perhaps there is something I could assist you with today? I'm Mr. McCoy and Mr. Syrias's personal assistant." She walked closer.

The man was abrupt, and add in his facial expression filled with annoyance and his dark hair and dark eyes, she found herself looking down to catch her breath and regain some confidence. When she looked back up, his eyes roamed over her body then returned to her eyes. He gave a small smirk.

"Very nice." He licked his lips, giving Brighid the creeps.

"But that won't be necessary. I'll meet up with them later." He stared at her for a few uncomfortable moments, and then Brighid gave him the once-over before walking away. She just wondered why she felt such an uneasy feeling for the stranger, as though she shouldn't turn her back on him at all.

Two hours later, Brighid leaned back in her chair and rubbed her temples. She could feel a small stress headache brewing. One look at the clock and she was shocked to see she was well past her normal hours. The last file she was working on had been red-flagged by other sources. Sometimes in fire investigation incidents, if numbers didn't add up or the investigation left questions, money could be withheld from the client until those red-flagged items were resolved. She'd spent the last few hours working on such a case, but all seemed to be fixed now.

She logged off of her computer and became aware of her bosses' voices in the office. It was so quiet. The other staff members had left, but she was so absorbed in resolving the case to close it and move on that she'd barely noticed every had left.

The voices grew louder, and she knew they were arguing. Lenny and Ray hardly ever fought, but lately she could sense their uneasiness. She figured it had to do with the transfer to New Jersey from Connecticut and the additional clientele they'd picked up. Perhaps they were growing too quickly?

The door suddenly opened just as she bent down to grab her bag.

"Don't walk away. Not after we get a letter like this and the phone calls," Lenny yelled at Ray from inside the room.

Ray locked gazes with Brighid just as Lenny came out after him.

"Brighid, so sorry, we didn't know you were still here," Ray said to her.

"I lost track of the time. That Parker case had me boggled down all day, but it's resolved now. I'll close it out tomorrow morning." She placed the strap of her bag onto her shoulder.

"What case did you say?" Lenny asked her.

"The Parker case from Connecticut where that fire took out most of the storefront mall. There were some red flags brought up along the investigation and unanswered questions by investigators, things like that. I called them up, straightened it all out."

"Oh, okay, great. See you tomorrow morning then?"

"Yes."

"Oh, I know the rest of the staff doesn't get in here until nine tomorrow, so why don't you do the same? You've been coming in extra early every morning and leaving extra late. That can't be good for your social life," Lenny said to her.

"What social life?" she said and chuckled.

"A beautiful woman like you should be out having fun, going on dates. I hear there are a lot of fun places in town." Lenny looked her over.

She didn't know why, but it made her feel kind of creeped out. Especially when Ray looked at her that way, too. In the past few years working for them, they'd never hit on her, so why would they now? It was odd, but since sleeping with those two firefighters, she felt almost guilty if another man flirted with her. That was pretty crazy, and she needed to get over those types of feelings fast.

"My friends and I will be going out this weekend. Thank God tomorrow is Friday. Have a good night," she said, wanting to get out of there.

"You, too, sweetheart," Ray said, and when she looked over her shoulder as she left, she caught both men checking her out. Weird. So very weird.

* * * *

"What are we going to do? He's fucking threatening us. He wants more money," Ray said to Lenny the second Brighid was out the door.

"I told you we're not paying him. He can fucking hold off until we need him for another job," Lenny replied.

"You know what, Lenny? You may not want to take his threats too lightly. He did do some major fucking jobs for us. He could bring us down, report us, and we could lose everything and wind up in jail.

Just return his calls and pay him something to keep his mouth shut and keep him hungry for more work."

"Not unless I have to. This guy doesn't scare me. What's he going to do to us? I'll take my chances. Guaranteed, he's bluffing. He can wait a little longer. I need to seal these deals with the clients, or there won't be any money to make."

* * * *

He could feel his heart racing. He couldn't believe it. It was immediate, the moment he'd locked onto her gorgeous red hair and then those green eyes. An angel of fire. She was special, sweet, yet had a toughness about her, which alerted him to new possibilities and their connection. She felt it, too, but ignored it. She insisted upon trying to help him when the other annoying secretary didn't know shit about helping people. He knew he'd taken a huge risk coming to the office, and he had gone back and forth contemplating the move to put the pressure on Ray and Lenny, but obviously there was a higher power at work here. The redhead was made for him. He felt it in every fiber of his body. He was on alert. He wanted her with him, and she was nothing like the others. He wanted her. The excitement filled his body.

He gripped the steering wheel and watched her. He needed to find out more about her. A chance encounter, a playful meeting somewhere. Something before she got away.

It was late. She would probably head home, which wouldn't be a bad thing, but he would have no reason to follow her to her house. She would call the cops. No, he needed to think rationally. He held his head but stared at the building. It was getting later and later. Could she be involved with Lenny and Ray? Could they be screwing her right there in the office after hours? He became enraged. *No. They can't be. She's too special. I felt it. She's mine.*

He banged the steering wheel and knew he needed to act fast.

He looked around the parking lot. No one was there. He made his way across the street. There were only three cars, and he knew which belonged to Ray and Lenny. The small, beat-up convertible had to be hers.

He looked around again and then pressed the knife into the tire. Not too much, just enough to slowly lose air and allow her to get farther away from the building where he could make physical contact with her again.

He smiled, closing the knife and heading back to his car. He would be sure to be the Good Samaritan that changed her flat tire and got to know her better while he made some plans. This move, this situation, was looking brighter than ever. Things appeared to working in his favor after all.

* * * *

Investigator Jeffrey Stone and Investigator Gregory Voight of the Connecticut State Police were formulating some possible leads into what they believed to be a series of connected homicides. Along with the local authorities, arson investigation team, and bureau of criminal investigative unit, they finally seemed to have some concrete evidence that linked the murders and a recent fire.

"So let me get this straight. You've analyzed the accelerant in the four homicides, as well as the two fires at the retail store and the car explosion in the garage, and they match?" Investigator Stone asked the lab coordinator at the state police forensics lab. His partner, Gregory, as well as an investigator in the arson unit, was with him.

"Yes, sir. It's a perfect match from what the testing has shown, indicating precisely the same chemicals used, which are not found in any common, over-the-counter products. It's a homemade formula, so dangerous to combine that the person would need to have knowledge of each of these chemicals and risk causing an explosion while combining them. The thing about the chemical this individual created is that it leaves a light coating of a white substance. That's what the arson investigators were able to find and get samples of."

"So this white substance, the remnants from the chemical used, was also collected and found at the other sites?" Gregory asked.

"Yes, sir. The forensics arson technician should be commended because this is like finding a needle in a haystack. It could appear just like ash, a white powdery substance with black soot around the edges." She reached for the file next to the one she had open and opened that one.

Jeffrey immediately saw the pictures of the victim burned to death. The coroner had stated the flesh was burned prior to the room being set on fire, and it had obviously been done to destroy evidence.

"We also matched the same chemical substance on the clothing remnants of the victims in the last three cases you felt were linked because of the MO. I'm currently getting a hold of the material sampled from previous female arson victims around Connecticut that you believed could be linked. So far, three others contain that same white substance, and my technicians are running those through testing. I should know within the day if the same chemical was used on the others."

"Holy shit. This is great news," Investigator Voight told her.

"Do you have a list of the chemicals so we can look into where a person can get these things?" Jeffrey asked.

"Sure do." She handed him a copy.

"You can't buy the chemicals in regular stores, but there are sites online, and you can have it shipped right to your home."

"Shit, that doesn't sound like it will be easy to track," the arson investigator said.

"No, but as we continue to look into these women who were burned and murdered, we might be able to find that one link, that person they all knew and, from there, who that person was and where they are now. We've got our work cut out for us, but now that the other few cases are linked, we can get all the info on those women and start looking for the connection. Let's move. I want to find this asshole before some other beautiful redhead gets killed," Jeffrey said, and they all agreed and headed out of the lab.

* * * *

"Thanks for picking me up," Pat told Tobin as he got into the truck. "The truck is all finished. Mercury and Frank said it needed a new power steering hose. They ordered it in and should have the truck ready by seven tomorrow morning."

Pat was in uniform from the police department, and Tobin still had on his dress pants, badge, and gun from working, too.

"It's not a problem. I was working late on a case."

"Anything interesting?" Pat asked him.

Tobin shook his head. "It's been going on for months. Just as we get close to our suspect, some new information arises and makes it seem like there's more people involved. I'm hoping for an arrest by next week, if not sooner."

Pat chuckled. "I hope so, too. Maybe you'll be able to make it to the Station with us Saturday night for some college ball?"

"Sounds good to me. I'm sure I'll need the break by then. Are Reece and Rusty off from work?"

"I think so. We'll have to check with them."

"Hey, you see that over there," Tobin said to Pat.

Across the way, there was a beat-up convertible with hazards on, and it looked like the tire was going flat.

"Yep. Flat tire."

As they slowed down, his brother made the U-Turn and came back around. Just as he approached, he saw another car pull up.

"Good Samaritan is going to help," Pat said just as Tobin flipped on the police lights.

A woman got out of the convertible, and her long red hair whipped around in the wind. The car that had slowed down stepped on the gas and took off.

"Guess not. Looks like we're the Good Samaritans," Tobin said and put the car in park, and they both got out.

"Got some car trouble?" Pat asked.

As the woman walked by the tire, dressed in a sexy business dress that showed off one hell of a body, Pat heard the horn honk, looked over his shoulder, and saw a sports car cut off a truck. The truck swerved, and Tobin grabbed Pat and the woman, pulling them to the side. Pat grabbed the woman tight, heard her scream, and then the truck whizzed by, clipping the side mirror of her car.

"Jesus! Are you both okay?" Tobin asked.

Pat nodded.

"Miss, are you okay?" he asked her, still holding her close as he looked down into the most beautiful green eyes he'd ever seen. She looked shocked and about ready to cry.

"Oh God, you both saved me. They would have killed us. God."

He felt her shaking. He caressed her arms, and Tobin was calling into his cell phone, giving license plate numbers and the make of the car and the truck.

Pat couldn't believe how beautiful the woman was.

"Are you all right?" he asked again, and she nodded.

"I'm sorry. Holy God, that was crazy."

She pulled back, and he didn't let her go a moment. She was stunning, and he wanted to know more about her.

"Uhm, you're a police officer?" she asked him, and he gave a soft smile and released her. "Just got off duty. My brother Tobin, he's a detective, picked me up because my truck is in the shop. Looks like you got a flat tire."

She nodded. Tobin was putting out safety flares.

He approached as she and Pat looked at the tire.

"You should stay in your vehicle when you have car troubles. Especially on a highway like this. That guy could have killed you," he said to her as he approached. But the woman blinked as if she were shocked by his abrupt tone.

She looked Tobin over. "So this is my fault?" she asked with attitude.

"No, my brother isn't saying that. He just got a bit frazzled like we did. We'll help you change the tire," Pat told her.

"I don't have a spare. I'll just call a tow truck."

"I've got a number of a friend," Pat said to her.

"You don't have a spare?" Tobin said.

She shook her head.

"Why the hell not? What if you were stranded on the side of the road somewhere and no help was coming? A young woman could get herself in quite the predicament if unprepared for emergencies," Tobin said, reprimanding her.

She lifted her phone, shook it, and gave him a wise-ass expression that had Pat covering his mouth to stifle a laugh.

"What do you call this? For your information, buddy, I used the spare tire a few weeks ago, but I just moved here with a job transfer and haven't gotten around to getting a new spare. And don't worry. I know how to change a tire," she snapped at him and then looked at Pat.

"You said you know a tow truck service? Can I get the number?" she asked Pat.

"I'll call for you," Pat said and then gave her a smile. She smiled back but then looked at Tobin, who absolutely towered over her, and she gave him an annoyed look. Pat couldn't get over it. He also wondered why his brother was being so hard on her.

* * * *

Tobin was shocked at the attitude, never mind the beauty, of the redhead they pulled over to help. One look at her gorgeous green eyes and long red hair and, of course, the snug-fitting business dress she had on and he was shocked at his body's response. She was sexy, classy, and, Jesus, built like a woman aiming to please. He was a big guy, and she was petite, and she smelled so good it was hard not to stand closer to her to get a better whiff. It was so carnal and wild to feel like this about a stranger. He was still shaken up a bit about her and Pat nearly getting killed by that truck driver, and now it seemed his attitude pissed her off. Well, he wasn't exactly a friendly guy, so what the fuck?

"He can't get out here for about an hour. He said lock it up, and you can come by tomorrow morning for it," Pat said to her.

She worried her bottom lip.

"Uhm, that's okay. I should figure something else out. I don't know the guy or you for that matter. I don't feel comfortable leaving it here. I guess I'll wait or maybe try Googling another tow service."

She looked down at her phone, and Pat covered her hand. She froze in place and Tobin watched, finding his brother's attraction to her interesting. Seemed he wasn't the only one affected by this knockout redhead.

"Don't be crazy. I'm a cop here in town. The name is Pat. My brother Tobin, is a detective. How much safer could you feel? We've known these guys with the tow service for years. This is what they do. So if Freddy, Frank's main guy, says an hour, he'll be here in an hour. You and I can exchange numbers. I'll give you his number, and we'll coordinate you picking up your car from him in the morning. I'll even go there, too, so you feel safe." He winked.

Her cheeks turned a nice shade of red, and Tobin watched the tip of her pink tongue slip from between her lips and lick the lower one, and then she sealed her lips. It was so damn sexy his cock hardened in his pants.

"She'll need a ride to her place and then in the morning unless you have a way of getting to the garage," Tobin added, now wanting to learn more about this woman, maybe get her number and ask her to meet them for drinks.

She looked around. "No taxi service around here?"

"You don't need one. You've got your own pair of law enforcement officers to keep you safe and get you home in one piece."

She looked at Pat's nametag. "Well, Officer McQuinn, I guess I should be thankful that you and your brother were driving by. Let me just get my bags and lock up the car."

Tobin watched her walk back to her car and open the passenger side of the door. Pat gave him a wink, and Tobin couldn't help but feel a little excited. But with their luck being so bad, he wouldn't be one bit surprised at all if this woman had a boyfriend. There was no possible way she was single. No way.

* * * *

"So, what's your name?" the big guy asked her as she got into the back seat of the car.

She didn't want to give her name. She was trying to be cautious. She could just show up at the garage tomorrow and tell him her real name. God, she was nervous. Two officers. Well, one police officer and one detective and both incredibly hot. She felt an instant attraction to them. Well, maybe not so much the detective and his bad attitude, but then as they started talking, it seemed as if he was a nice guy, too. He had been shaken up at seeing his brother nearly get run over by a truck because she had a flat tire. She felt guilty, but as they told her about the town and gave her a ride home to her condominium complex, she absorbed more about them.

Both men were super sexy with muscles and were very tall and handsome. It was kind of funny because she instantly thought about her two firemen, Reece and Rusty. Her fireman? She had some nerve thinking of them in that way. Yet, she couldn't stop thinking about them. She didn't even know where they came from or lived, and here she was in a new town and attracted to two other men, first responders, too, and boy, did she feel kind of crappy. Had doing a one-night stand suddenly made her feel as though she could do it again and with these two? *Damn, I'm losing my mind. I must be desperate to feel like I did with Reece and Rusty and I'm projecting that attraction, that desire, into these two strikingly handsome men who rescued me.*

Shit, I'm turning into a lust-crazed slut, ready to have sex with any man I meet who I feel this attracted, too. But I've never felt so attracted to men like this. First the two firefighters and now these two? What are the chances? Am I just tired of being lonely?

"Are you okay?" Pat asked her.

"Oh, yes, sorry, it was a long day at work. It's Bri."

"Where do you work?" Tobin asked.

"An insurance company. We just moved the business from Connecticut a couple of weeks ago. I've been working such long hours. I sure didn't need this flat tire tonight."

"Well, if you need a ride in the morning, we could work it out," Pat offered. "I don't have to be in until eleven, and I'm picking up my truck at seven when Tobin heads into work."

"That's so sweet of you, Pat. Thanks for your kindness. I only know a few people around here, but the town seems very friendly."

"Oh, it is friendly." He turned to look at her. "Now that I have your number and you have mine, if you ever need anything, don't hesitate to call me."

She felt her cheeks warm and nodded.

Tobin cleared his throat. "This is a brand new complex. How do you like it?"

"Oh, I love it so far. I haven't had time for the amenities, but hopefully over the next few weekends, I can take a little break."

"I heard the condos are really big and the ones on the beach side have outstanding views."

"Oh they do. It's so gorgeous."

Tobin pulled into the front parking lot.

"We'll walk you up," Pat said, and before she could tell him it was okay, Pat was closing the passenger door and opening up her door.

He took her office bag and placed it on his shoulder then offered his hand for her to take, and he assisted her out of the truck. She hoped she looked sexy as her dress skirt lifted mid thigh and she saw his eyes look down and then back into her eyes.

He was very attractive with crew cut brown hair that was slicked up in front. His forearm muscles were large, too, and he had rolled up his uniform sleeves, showing off those cords of muscles to his large hands.

She got out and fixed her dress then heard the other door close.

She placed her bag on her shoulder. "You really don't have to walk me up."

"Are you kidding? We want to check out the raves about this place." Pat placed his hand at her lower back and guided her along the path in front of the car and to the main entrance.

"Oh, so you're using me," she said to him as Tobin opened the door and held her gaze.

"No, of course not," Pat said, but she couldn't laugh because Tobin was staring at her with such a serious, hard expression she felt both nervous and entirely too turned on to be normal.

His dark eyes told so much. He wasn't a trusting man. He was hard. Maybe he'd had a hard life or tough experiences. Maybe it was his profession. Being a detective had to be difficult.

"Good evening, Miss Murphy. Is everything okay?" Clark, the front door man, asked her as he looked at Pat and Tobin.

"Oh, yes, Clark, thank you. This is Officer McQuinn and his brother, Detective McQuinn. I got a flat tire on the highway, and they gave me a ride home."

"Oh, how terrible. You know you can call here if anything like that ever happens again. We have people around the community that could get to you fast."

"That's so nice of you, Clark, but thank goodness a police officer and detective were there to help. Have a good night. They'll be down in a few minutes, just so you know."

Clark nodded as she, Pat, and Tobin got into the elevator.

The doors closed, and both men had their arms crossed in front of their chests.

They were quiet.

"What's wrong?" she asked Pat. He didn't say anything.

"I was only kidding about the using me comment," she added, thinking that was what had insulted him.

"That guy Clark likes you. You should be careful, especially being new in town," Tobin said, kind of forcefully.

"I don't think so. He's nice to everyone."

"Bri, not every place that has a doorman offers to come to your aid if you're not in the complex. He was hinting that he has an interest in you," he said to her, and she felt badly for lying about her name, for one, and she felt kind of confused about Clark and not getting that feeling from him. But then it was all overpowered by the fact that obviously Pat felt jealous, as did Tobin. How the hell had this happened? Maybe she shouldn't have allowed them to walk her up.

The elevator chimed, and the doors opened on the eighth floor. Pat motioned for her to lead the way, and she did. She unlocked her door to a corner unit that was extralarge and looked out over the ocean with a wraparound balcony.

As soon as they walked in, she hit the lights.

"Whoa," Pat said and walked all the way inside.

"Look around. I'll take the bag," she said to him, and he handed it to her and took in the sight. Tobin did, too, walking through the open floor plan and kitchen area, past a wet bar to the wall-to-wall sliding doors, which led to the wide balcony.

"You can check it out," she said, walking across the floor, her heels clicking along the way. She unlocked the sliders, and they stepped out onto the balcony.

"Damn, Bri, this is gorgeous," Tobin told her. She looked at both men as she leaned against the doorframe. She felt the attraction getting stronger, but she wouldn't make the same mistake she'd made weeks ago.

"How many bedrooms does it have?" Pat asked, walking close to her and brushing his arm against her side as they stood in the doorway. He pressed a little closer than necessary, but she didn't mind one bit. He smelled so damn good, and she could imagine how hard all those muscles on him were.

"Two bedrooms, a smaller room like an office, and a very large bathroom. It has one of those Jacuzzi tubs in it that can fit like five people."

He squinted at her and held her gaze. "Five, huh?"

"I like that number," Tobin said as he passed through.

She didn't know what their comment meant, but she followed them as they checked out the kitchen and then waked down the hallway to the bedrooms.

"My God, this is like nothing I've ever seen before," Pat told her.

She smiled. "I was completely impressed when I first got here and saw it. But my bosses set the whole thing up and paid for it, for the first year anyway. I take it over after that if I want to stay."

"You're thinking of leaving?" Tobin asked, walking back over toward her and leaning against the dresser with his arms crossed. She felt kind of weird having a conversation with these two sexy men in her bedroom. Throw in the uniforms, the way they were both armed and so attractive, muscular, and very comfortable there, she knew she needed to get her act together and stop drooling.

She cleared her throat. "No, it's just this isn't really my style. I like simpler things, not so glam and ritzy. I don't know."

She turned to walk out of the bedroom. They followed, and the closer she got to the door, the more relaxed she felt.

"Well, I appreciate all your help tonight and for saving my life." She stood near the wall by the door.

Pat placed his hand on the wall over her shoulder and got closer to her. She went to move her hands, which were behind her back as she used them to lean back, but couldn't.

He caressed a strand of hair from her cheek. "How about you really make our night and say yes to meeting us for a drink one night?"

He heart hammered. Why she felt guilty she couldn't explain.

"I really can't."

"Why not?" Tobin pushed in that forceful, demanding tone of his. She looked over at him now that he stood right beside Pat, so close to her other side, making her feel caged in but also very affected.

"I really don't date."

"Why? Bad experience?" Pat asked as he placed his hand on her hip.

"Something like that."

"Well, think about it. Maybe give me an answer tomorrow when I pick you up to bring you by the garage."

"You don't have to do that, Pat," she told him, and he smiled.

"But I want to see you again. So does Tobin."

Her eyes widened, and she looked at Tobin, still wearing that serious expression.

"We'll be at the Station near the boardwalk, Saturday from five o'clock on. Meet us there. You can bring some friends, too, if you feel safer."

"Oh, like to meet you and some other friends?" she asked.

Pat clutched her chin, and she totally focused on him.

"Oh, there's something you should know about us."

She swallowed hard.

"We like to share, and that means everything," Tobin said. Her lips parted, and Pat brushed his thumb along her lower lip.

"I would love to kiss you right now, and so would Tobin, but I don't want to scare you. You trusted us enough to let us walk you upstairs. Trust the attraction you feel for both of us and join us at the Station on Saturday."

She looked from Tobin to Pat, feeling aroused and overwhelmed at the same time. What were the chances that two ménage encounters could be offered weeks apart? If this went somewhere, if she could forget about Reece and Rusty and the amazing time and connection she had with them, maybe something with Tobin and Pat could happen and mean something real. Could she take that chance and possibly make a huge mistake?

"Come on and say yes," he pushed. "I'll pick you up for the ride tomorrow morning at eight, okay?"

"Okay, but let me think about Saturday."

"Hope you say yes, Bri," Tobin said, and Pat stepped back, brought her hand up to his lips, and kissed the top.

"See you in the morning. Thanks for the tour."

He winked, and she opened the door and watched them leave. She closed the door, locked it, and leaned against it.

"Holy shit. I can't believe it's happening again. If I do go Saturday, I'm staying away from the tequila, no matter what Jenny and the others say."

Chapter 3

He watched her from across the street. She was smiling and laughing with that dick who'd helped her with her car last night. That should have been him. He was the one who'd slashed her tire. He was supposed to show up and rescue her. He slammed his hand down on the steering wheel. The dick couldn't keep his hands off of her. He offered her a hand to get out of his truck then caught her as she nearly fell from the seat because the truck was so high. He'd taken advantage of the move, pulling Brighid close to his body and staring down into her gorgeous green eyes as she held on to his forearms.

"Fuck. She's mine. All mine, you fucking dick, whoever you are." He felt his temper rise, as if his blood boiled within his veins. That fucking cop better think twice about going after her. Cops were always having accidents. It would be a shame if the Good Samaritan had one, too.

He gripped the steering wheel tighter. How had he become so instantly obsessed with her? She was so different from the others. None of them compared to her beauty or to the power of her presence. He watched her. She had a sexy figure. He could imagine having her in his bed, tied up, arms stretched above her head, legs wide and tied to the posts. He could take her anytime, anywhere, he wanted. He'd saved enough money to be able to live without working for quite some time. She would be his pet, the symbol of his talent, and she would beg for his touch. Beg for the touch of the flame against her skin that only he could place against her. In the darkness, with only the light of the flame in her sight, with no shadows of light to take away her fear or lessen his control, he would show her his power and the burning of the flame. But unlike the others, where he'd gone too far, their shrill screams pulling them away from the meaning behind the flame and his decision to touch them in that way, Brighid would prevail. She would survive the test of fire. They would become one in hearts and souls and in bodies. His mark, the mark of the power of light, more powerful than God, than Stark himself, would be imprinted on her skin forever. He needed to make some plans. He had a job to do for Lenny and Ray, but then he would be taking his prize and disappearing forever.

* * * *

Brighid couldn't believe the attraction she felt for Pat. He had a great personality to boot, and every chance he had to touch her, brush against her, or smile at her, he did it. He was a charmer, and she knew, when her friends met him and Tobin, they were going to go crazy, too.

She had spoken to Jenny about how she'd met them and what she was feeling. That guilty sensation wouldn't go away. It was the oddest thing. She'd met Reece and Rusty and knew so little about them yet felt a bond had formed. She was definitely losing her mind, and maybe exploring this attraction to Pat and Tobin might bring her back to reality.

She placed her pocketbook strap onto her shoulder and walked along the pathway to get inside of the service station. Her car was sitting in a parking spot, and she could see the one new tire.

When they walked into the office, a really attractive guy was standing there already reaching his hand out to greet Pat. He was a big guy, too.

"Hey, Pat, how are you, buddy?"

Pat shook the man's hand as the man gave her the once-over and smiled.

"So this must be Bri." He reached his hand out to her next.

"It sure is. Bri, meet my friend Kyle St. James."

"Hello, Kyle. It's nice to meet you. Thank you so much for taking care of my car," she told him as she shook his hand. He smiled and then crossed his arms in front of his large chest.

"No problem. I noticed that your side mirror was broken. If you wanted me to fix that, I can order the part and have it here in a day or so."

"Oh God, I totally forgot about that. My focus was on the fact that Pat and Tobin saved my life."

He squinted at her and looked at Pat. "What happened?

Pat explained about seeing her on the side of the road with tire problems and about the sports car that had cut off the truck that nearly hit her and, instead, got so close it scraped against her mirror.

"Damn, you could have been killed," Kyle said. "All three of you could have gotten hurt. That's terrible. But I bet Tobin will track down that truck and the sports car."

"I'm sure he will, too. My brother can be a pit bull when it comes to things like that. He won't give up until he gets the results he wants."

"Well, you keep me posted on that and, of course, let me know if you want me to order that part."

"Sounds good to me. I'll need it, so that would be great. I can give you my card, and when it comes in, call me and I'll schedule an appointment with you." She reached into her bag. She pulled out a business card and handed it to Kyle.

"Great. I'll call you when it comes in. Let me get the keys to your car."

"Oh, let me pay you. How much do I owe you?" She followed him toward the counter. He pulled out a bill, and she paid cash then got the receipt.

"Thank you again."

They all shook hands, and Pat held the door open and escorted her to her car. He never let his hand off her lower back, and when she got to her car and turned around, he placed his hands on her hips.

He stared down into her eyes. His gorgeous brown eyes held her gaze, and she could tell he was just as in tune to the attraction between them as she was.

"Did I tell you how sexy and classy you look in this dress?" he asked, letting his eyes roam over her cleavage, which was accentuated by the snug-fitting bodice of the Ann Taylor navy blue dress she wore.

She was grateful for the matching high heels, as Pat was a good foot taller than her.

"Thank you," she replied, voice cracking.

"I'm looking forward to spending some time with you on Saturday. So is Tobin."

She smiled. "I told my friends about the place. They were coming to stay overnight at my place, so they'll be arriving Friday night."

"Nice. They're from Connecticut too?"

"Yes, but they've been job hunting and looking to head south. I'm hoping they like Treasure Town and can find work here or nearby and move here. We've been friends since high school."

"That's great. How many friends will be staying with you?"

"Four of them. Jenny, Anna, Carmella, and Natalie."

"I can't wait to meet them. I bet they'll love The Station, too." He gently glided his finger along her chin and jaw. He tilted her chin up toward him.

"We seriously need to get this first date out of the way. It's just too difficult to not want to kiss you."

She felt her cheeks warm. "Is that what Saturday is? A first date?"

"It's a start, so you can get to know us. You're definitely coming there, right?" he asked.

She nodded. "I'll be there, Pat. I promise."

He smiled and then leaned forward and kissed her forehead. She inhaled his cologne, placed her hands on his waist, and so badly wished she could have felt his lips against hers. But then he stepped back.

"I'll call you to touch base."

"Okay. Bye, oh, and have a nice day. Be safe out there."

"You, too." He winked as he opened her door, and she got inside. He closed it, stepped back a bit, and waited for her to start the car and then pull out of the parking lot.

As she headed onto the main road, she glanced into the rearview mirror and saw him watching her, smiling and then shaking his head as he headed toward his truck.

She couldn't help but feel that giddy, exciting feeling in her belly. But she was surprised when her mind immediately went to thoughts of Rusty and Reece. That had been truly something special between the three of them, but more than likely, she would never see them again. She couldn't hold out and not explore other attractions. Not when men like Tobin and Pat drew her in and aroused her body and senses just as strongly as Reece and Rusty had. What were the chances? Maybe this was God's way of giving her another chance. Who knows, but no matter what, she was going to make sure she stayed sober and wound up in her own bed Sunday morning. She chuckled and then turned up the radio and made her way to work.

* * * *

"You promise that I won't get caught? That however you pull this off I'll get the money I need?" Bricker Daily asked Lenny when they met at the convenience store parking lot.

"We've worked this out before. You'll be just fine. All bases are covered. Just sign the documents securing us as your insurance agents and confirming the policy is intact. Your verbal, promise to give us our cut is good enough, and it will be great."

"And no one will get hurt, right? I don't want any of my employees to get injured. I never thought the business would fail like this and I would have to resort to doing something this illegal. You're certain the arson investigators won't be able to figure shit out?"

Lenny gave a soft smile. "If you go down, and our guy goes down, so do we. And, keep in mind, we have major money invested in this company. We'd lose everything."

"Okay. I'll do it." Bricker signed the contract. He handed it over to Lenny, and Lenny folded it up and then got down to business.

"You don't say a word to anyone ever about this. Stop in the office today. I'll have papers waiting for you to sign with our secretary, Brighid. She'll get those into the system, and you give that down payment of the year's insurance cost up-front. You're already put you in the system as a client for the past three years. Martha, one of our new employees, won't know the difference because she just started."

"But I never paid anything. There isn't a paper trail."

"In the computer there is. When your account shows only this recent check and then bogus numbers for other checks, Martha will think it's some sort of glitch on the system. She's new. That's why the opportunity is now. Don't worry about an arson investigation. It's not going to get that far. When they do an inquiry, if they feel it is a suspicious fire, it takes time, and they don't look for the paper trail until later, but the computer files will cover that. I'm telling you that my guy is that good. No worries."

Bricker ran his fingers through his hair.

"God, I don't know about this. I'm a nervous wreck. I've got my kids to worry about and my wife."

"That's why we talked about this as an option. Another few months and you'll be missing payment dates on bills and red-flagging yourself across the board. Right now you're squeezing by. When this pay-off comes through, you can keep the gift shop open, expand it, or simply retire. Your choice. I need to get moving. Drop those papers and the check off today."

"Okay. Later."

As Lenny walked away, he thought about the payments and paper trail. He would log into Brighid's computer and change some things. He could make up a few other check numbers and account information. She wouldn't notice a thing and definitely not from three years ago up to the current payment Bricker handed in today since he would fall under Martha's list of clients and Martha was new. Maybe getting this job would get Stark, as he liked to be called, off their asses. They would be rolling in a pretty big payoff. He needed to adjust those numbers and call Ray. This would work out just fine.

* * * *

Jenny, Anna, Carmella, and Natalie arrived around seven in the evening Friday night. They were raring to go and already talking about how good looking the men around the town were. They unpacked their bags spread out around the living room as Jenny called dibs on the bedroom.

They were on their second bottle of wine as they got ready and tried to decide where to go tonight.

"So tell us about this place we're going tomorrow," Carmella said.

"Tell us about the two sexy cops you met that you're meeting there. You're on a roll with landing some hotties," Jenny teased.

"I am not." She gave Jenny a scolding expression in warning. After all, Brighid was sworn to secrecy about Jenny's one-night stand with some sexy cop, just as Jenny was sworn to secrecy about Brighid's ménage encounter, although that was all they seemed to talk about lately. It seemed Jenny couldn't get the cop she slept with off her mind, just like Brighid couldn't stop thinking about the two firefighters.

She explained about how they'd met and talked about having some reservations.

"Why? They sound delicious, and you're single, so what gives?" Anna asked her.

"I don't know. It's two men, a ménage. That's crazy stuff."

"Sounds sexy as damn hell to me. I wouldn't mind grabbing a few firefighters or a few cops to take to bed," Carmella stated, and they chuckled.

"You're so full of crap. You're completely shy, hardly even date, and never even had a one-night stand. You're a goody-goody," Natalie added.

Anna, Jenny, and Brighid laughed.

"Well, maybe she's ready to live a little. Give her a break. Maybe she'll meet some men tonight or tomorrow night at the Station, and have her fling and party weekend," Jenny said.

"Sounds like a plan to me." Anna raised her wine glass. They made a toast to having a good time and to their friendship.

"So what happens if you want to hook up with your two cop friends tomorrow Brighid? Are we kicked out of here, or will you go to their place?" Carmella asked and took a sip of wine.

Brighid felt her chest tighten, but she knew she wouldn't sleep with them. Not tomorrow anyway. She felt guilty enough about sleeping with two amazing men she didn't know and trying to process why she still felt compelled to think about them and to feel guilty. She didn't need to sleep with another two men she hardly knew only because there was a strong attraction. Well, a very strong one.

"Don't worry. I'm not going to sleep with them. I don't really know them."

"Well, if you change your mind, give the most responsible woman and least drunk one the keys to this place, and we'll kick back here until you return," Natalie said to her.

"What about the doorman? He was kind of weird and asked all these questions like how long we were staying and where we came from," Anna said.

"He's harmless. He just likes to keep a secure building. He'll let you in now that I introduced you. So what do you say? Go out and grab dinner and hit a hot spot or stay in, order food, and save all our energy for tomorrow night?" Brighid asked.

"Hell no, we're here to party. I saw a sign on the way in for a place called the Boathouse Bar and Restaurant. Have you been there?" Carmella asked.

"Not yet."

"There we go. Let's get ready and head out," Jenny said, and they all agreed and prepared for a fun-filled night like old times.

* * * *

"I'm telling you, Rusty, she is gorgeous. I mean really classy with long red hair and big green eyes, and she's petite. We hit it off with her so well." Pat took a slug from his beer bottle.

"Maybe it was just the whole saving-her-from-getting-run-over thing that has you two feeling this strongly about her," Reece said, and he seemed annoyed with them.

"Hey, we listened to you guys talk about the woman you met, slept with, and felt that there was a strong connection to. Bri is special, I'm telling you. Even Tobin likes her," Pat added.

Reece and Rusty looked at Tobin, who remained straight-faced.

"She's shy and probably won't even show up tonight. Her friends came in to join her last night, and they went out to the Boathouse and got back late. I wouldn't get your hopes up, Pat," Tobin said, sounding unsure.

Pat looked at his watch. It was nearly seven, and he was getting antsy. She was late. What if she didn't show up? What should he do? Call her?

He took out his cell phone and saw that there weren't any messages or missed calls.

Then they heard some laughter, and Pat looked up toward the front entryway near the bar and saw a group of women, all smiling and laughing, and he locked gazes with Bri.

Then Reece smacked Rusty's stomach. "Holy shit. That's her. That's Brighid."

They stood up.

"Which one?" Tobin asked.

"The redhead," Reece said, and Pat saw Bri's expression go from smiling to plain-out shocked as her eyes widened, she stopped walking and just gaped at them. She grabbed one friend's arm, and her friend looked at her, then at them, and her mouth dropped open, too. Bri turned around and headed out the door.

"What the fuck is going on? Where is she going? She had to have seen us," Reece said as he, Rusty, Tobin, and Pat headed toward the entrance.

"Your Brighid is our Bri?" Tobin asked, sounding angry.

Pat chuckled. "Holy shit, we met the same woman and all are attracted to her."

They all started walking by the crowd of women so they could find Brighid.

"Um, hold it right there. Where do you think you're going?" her friend asked, trying to block them.

"Don't even try it, honey. We saw her. We've been going crazy thinking about her," Reece told her friend.

"Really?" the woman asked as Reece, Rusty, and Tobin left there to find Bri.

"Yes, really, and it seems our brothers met her, too, here in town and hit it off."

Her friend's eyes widened and then formed into a huge smile.

"Holy crap, then go get her, but she's embarrassed about what happened. She never did anything like that before. She's had crappy boyfriends, and she drank too much that night but totally didn't regret it."

Pat smiled. "Thanks, honey, and don't worry. My brothers and I will treat her real good."

Pat ran outside and looked both ways. He saw his brothers all standing near the sidewalk and a bench. He hurried over.

* * * *

Brighid was so embarrassed she wanted to cry and just let the ground open up and swallow her whole. How embarrassing? Her heart pounded inside of her chest. Two men she'd slept with, had a one-night stand with, were at the same place, hanging out with the two newest men she was attracted to. What were the odds? *Really? Fucking really? Something like this can only happen to me.*

She covered her face and just sat there. There was no place to go. Pat and Tobin knew where she lived, and she and the girls had taken a taxi to get to the place because they couldn't all fit in her small car and her friends planned on drinking.

She felt the presence of all four large men as they stood around her. They probably hated her, thought she was a slut. She felt so dirty and low. Two men she'd slept with one night as she threw caution to the wind and followed her heart and her body's attraction to Reece and Rusty. Then there was Tobin and Pat. Oh God, Tobin was going to hate her, and Pat might, too. Then one of them bent down and placed his hand on her knee.

"Look at us, Brighid," he said, and she uncovered her face and stared at Rusty.

Dark hair, dark eyes, tattoos along his arm and wrist. He looked calm but serious. Her heart raced. He was so good looking. God, and his body? His body was to die for, and now he wore a sexy grin and one damn tight black T-shirt that showed off his muscles big time. She swallowed hard, wanting to smack herself because the sight of him made her breasts swell and her pussy throb. *Holy crap, I am a slut. I'm a sex-craved ho.*

The tears filled her eyes.

He gave a soft smile. "Damn, baby, we've been trying to find you. Now you just shocked the hell out of all of us."

"It's not what you think. Well, I mean it is. I mean I met Tobin and Pat. They saved me, and, well, we hit it off. Wait. Did you say you've been trying to find me?"

He chuckled and gave her knee another squeeze. She wished he would stop doing that. She couldn't concentrate. She went to reach up to touch him but then pulled back. She couldn't do that. Not with Tobin and Pat standing there.

"I can't believe you're here," he said to her.

"Me? What are you doing here in Treasure Town? How do you know Pat and Tobin?" She glanced up at them. Pat sat down next to her and smiled.

"I mean I just met them a few days ago. I had a flat tire, and then some car nearly ran us over," she started to explain as if she needed to make them understand that she wasn't cheating on them, but really, she sort of was in a way only because she felt guilty.

"We're brothers," Pat said.

"What?" She stood up, and Rusty and Reece stepped back.

"Oh my God. Oh God, this is so embarrassing. It's crazy." She covered her face again and felt as though she was on fire she was so embarrassed.

"Oh God, Oh God, oh God," she rambled and heard Pat chuckle. Then she felt his arm go around her waist from behind. He pressed up against her, and she tightened up. He kissed her shoulder.

"This shouldn't be embarrassing. It's perfect," Pat said to her.

She pulled from his hold, and Rusty took her hand and brought her close against his chest. He ran his hand along her waist to her lower back as he stared down into her eyes.

"It's crazy as damn hell but fucking perfect."

"You were made for us," Pat said very seriously.

She turned around to look at him and at Reece and Tobin, who looked intense to say the least.

She looked at Pat. "What?" she asked, raising her voice.

He looked at his brothers, and she glanced at them, Especially at Tobin and Reece who stood there with their arms crossed in front of their chests, looking pissed off with hard expressions and appearing shocked.

"Sit down, Brighid. Let's talk this through so we can get on with our date," Pat told her. She sat down on the bench Rusty knelt down next to her, and Pat took a seat next to her on the bench.

Rusty squeezed her knee and then began to run his hand along her thigh back and forth. "We haven't stopped thinking about you or that crazy, freaking night."

"Really?"

"Of course we haven't. We were so upset when we woke up in the morning and you were gone and we hadn't gotten your number. It's been hell thinking you moved to New Orleans," Reece told her.

She pulled her bottom lip between her teeth and squinted.

"I lied about that. I was worried about giving up too much information, and when the night went on and the tequila kicked in, I didn't bother to correct it. I never did anything like that before. The night was so perfect, and I really enjoyed your company."

"And we enjoyed yours." Rusty let his eyes linger lower over her breasts and then to her lips.

She felt them tingle with desire. She wished she could have remembered more about that night of making love to Reece and Rusty. Then she looked at Tobin.

"This is a total mess. You must think the worst of me. You should know that I never did anything like that before. That night was not normal. This is so wild, to meet four brothers separately and feel like this for all of you." She covered her mouth and stood up. She stepped away from them.

"What's wrong?" Rusty asked.

"Yeah, what you said is a good thing, baby. My brothers and I share everything," Pat told her.

"Your friend said that you couldn't stop thinking about us either and that you have strong feelings for Pat and Tobin too," Reece chimed in.

She opened her mouth to speak. Tobin stepped closer.

"I think we should just settle down and let the woman digest all of this."

He ran his hand along her waist and then pulled her close. He licked his lips and looked down into her eyes.

"A connection, an attraction like this one, does not come along too often at all. Why don't we head back inside where all your friends are waiting and enjoy the night getting to know one another together?"

Tobin was the voice of reason, a leader, the one man who, when he spoke, everyone listened to, including her. He was charismatic, hard, and so commanding that she found herself nodding slowly to his suggestion.

"You still want to get to know me? You don't think terrible things about me?" she asked, and his expression looked firm as he squinted his eyes. But then he shook his head and winked as he said, "Tsk, tsk." She felt a light bit of relief.

He didn't smile, but instead, he leaned closer and pressed his lips to hers as he pulled her snug against his body. She kissed him right back, and that kiss grew deeper, wilder, and full of lust and desire. He held her so close that she felt safe, secure and protected. When his palm moved along her thigh and over her ass, squeezing it, she didn't even pull away. She pressed closer and felt her breasts smush against his hard pectoral muscles until he slowly released her lips.

"I'm not letting you outta my sight tonight," he said very seriously, and she was shocked, aroused, intimidated until he gave a soft wink, took her hand, and led her back inside to the bar, along with his brothers. One look at her friends' big smiles when she walked back inside and she knew that this night was going to be just as wild and crazy as the night she'd met and slept with Reece and Rusty McQuinn.

* * * *

Rusty couldn't help but smile. Brighid absolutely lit up a room. From her striking red hair in waves along her shoulders to her gorgeous green eyes to her infectious laughter, she was beyond appealing. He noticed other men looking at her, and when she excused herself to go to the ladies room, men watched, checked her out, and even had the nerve to say hello. She was theirs. He had no doubt in his mind that Brighid was the woman who was made for him and his brothers.

He glanced at Tobin, badass, always on guard, always looking around waiting, anticipating some sort of situation being the detective he was. His brother rarely dated. When they asked him why, he always had an excuse. Too busy with work. A heavy case was on his mind. He didn't meet anyone worth dating. He had become somewhat cynical when it came to women and what they were after. Rusty figured it had to do with the one time they'd all been out and he'd seen a woman he'd slept with. She came over, flirted, led him on, and then went back to her friends and some guys she was chilling with. A while later, she came back over again and asked Tobin if it was true that he and his brothers liked to share. When he told her sometimes, she said she was more than willing to do him and his brothers, and Tobin had been pissed. He didn't want to be some fling, some adventure for a woman. Nor did Rusty and the rest of them.

Which was kind of like having a double standard. They only had a few ménage encounters, and they chose who to sleep with if they were into her. But he was getting older. His brothers lost interest in that and were all so busy lately. So he wondered why now, why with Brighid did things feel different than ever before?

This type of relationship was serious and involved a true commitment. That was what lacked in other sexual encounters. They learned by watching their friends that it could mean so much more and make them feel complete and like a family. He wanted that.

He looked at her again as she talked, and he saw the difference in his brothers' eyes as they spoke with her and in their body language. He felt it, too. It made Rusty wonder if Tobin was concerned about Brighid being the one for them because she'd slept with Rusty and Reece when she was drunk. Rusty had to admit that he worried about it too, but his gut clenched as he did, warning him that it wasn't the case. Brighid wasn't out for a good time, a quick fuck fest, an orgy. She was real. She truly had feelings for them, and she had the night they'd slept with her. He hadn't been the same man since.

"I'll be right back," Tobin said, his eyes glued to the back of the room where the hallway and the ladies room was. Apparently Tobin didn't like having Brighid out of his sight either.

* * * *

Brighid looked at her reflection in the mirror. Her cheeks were nice and rosy, her eyes glistening with desire. Her breasts felt fuller, her pussy needy. It was so crazy. Part of her just wanted to give in and go home with the four St. James men and explore these feelings. But a larger part of her felt unsure because this whole situation was crazy. This had to be the craziest of situations for a woman to engage in a one-night stand when drunk and actually have deep feelings for the men she'd slept with, only to make a run for it and wind up practically in the arms of said two men's brothers. Jesus, she couldn't make this shit up it was so unreal. Why had she drunk that tequila?

She looked at her reflection in the mirror, the swell of her breasts, the deep cleavage in the blouse she wore.

How the hell could this be happening? Four brothers?. They are incredible, and damn it, you like all four of them. They want you.

Her heart began to race as her mind competed with the sporadic thoughts. *I never imagined being involved in a ménage. Well, not a quadruple one, if that's what it's referred to as. Jesus.* She fanned her face and then turned on the cool water and pressed it to her cheeks before turning off the faucet, reaching for a towel, and blotting her cheeks.

What if they ask me to go home with them? I have my friends staying at my place. I couldn't do that. What would the girls think? Forget that. They were already asking for the key to her condo and telling her to go home with the St James brothers. Hell, every few seconds one of them was whispering in her ear with jealousy and comments about how fine the men were in all aspects of the word. She couldn't believe the jealous feelings she had knowing her friends were undressing the men with their eyes. *Get your own first responders.*

She scrunched her eyes together and then shook her head. She couldn't hide out in here much longer. They would think she'd taken off again.

She chuckled. God, that was a moment to remember.

She took a deep breath and then released it before pressing her palms down her short black skirt and looking at herself in the full-length mirror. Thank goodness she'd dressed to impress tonight.

As she walked out of the bathroom, she saw a man standing there waiting. She thought he looked familiar, and then he smiled.

"Brighid, wow, funny bumping into you here," he said, and then it hit her. She remembered him from the office the other day.

"Hi, I'm sorry, I don't think I got your name the other day."

He eyed her over then caught himself staring at her breasts, which totally creeped her out, and he reached his hand out.

"Stark."

She shook his hand and felt the odd vibes, especially when he didn't release her hand right away.

"You look beautiful. Do you come here a lot?"

"Thank you, and no, I don't. This is my first time. I'm here with friends." She decided to follow those gut instincts of hers and get back to her friends. After all, she had an odd feeling that he had seen her walk into the ladies room and was waiting for her to come out.

"Well, I should get back to my friends. Enjoy the evening." When she went to pass, he grabbed her wrist. She stopped short. He inhaled next to her. and she looked up into his dark grey eyes. A feeling of evilness, darkness fell over her body.

"I hope to see you again real soon."

She pulled away and walked right into Tobin.

His arms wrapped around her waist, and he hauled her close, his hand landing over her ass as he maneuvered her into position against his hip.

His eyes never left Stark's.

"Everything all right over here, baby?" he asked.

She placed her hand against Tobin's chest and could feel her heart racing. She was actually a little scared, and she didn't understand why.

Stark gave Tobin the once-over and then looked at her, almost giving her the evil eye.

"See you around, Brighid." He walked away. She watched him disappear into the crowd of people, and Tobin gripped her hips and held her in front of him.

"Who the hell was that?" he asked ,and she held on to his forearms.

"I don't really know him. I think he's one of the customers from work. He came in the other day, and I went to help him, and then he said he had to go."

"Does he have a name?"

"Stark. Why?"

"I didn't like the way he was looking at you."

She wondered if Tobin had seen Stark grab her wrist. She wasn't going to bring it up. Instead, she ran her hands up his chest and then lay her cheek against it. She felt so safe in his arms, especially as he ran his hands along her back, caressing it. Then he began to walk her backward.

"Tobin?"

He grabbed her hand, and they headed down the hallway and to the back exit. He pushed the door open and then pulled her into his arms. He kissed her deeply, and she kissed him back. It was wild, erotic, and the feel of his muscles beneath her fingertips, countering his hard, large hands exploring her body, squeezing her ass, and then cupping her breast drove her wild.

When his hand went up her skirt on the left side, the side facing the building, she tightened up. What if someone saw? But there was no one around. It wasn't even a parking lot or a garbage area. It was literally a side emergency exit.

His hand cupped her ass cheek and squeezed as he rocked his hips, his hard cock against her mound. He pulled from her mouth just as he ran a finger along the crack of her ass. The tip scalded her pussy.

"Oh God." She moaned. He suckled the skin of her neck and chin. She gripped his shoulders.

"You taste so fucking delicious. I want you, Brighid. I want you to come home with my brothers and I and be our woman."

"Oh, Tobin, God, this is insane. I can't. I shouldn't."

He stopped kissing her and gripped her tighter and gave her hips, her ass cheek, a shake.

"Why the hell not?" he demanded to know. His tone sounded as desperate for an answer as she felt for more of his kisses..

Her lips were parted, and she stared at his eyes, those dark brown eyes that were filled with emotion, lust, and desire for her.

"For lots of reasons."

"Name them," he pushed.

Why did it feel as though she was being interrogated? He would want answers. He was a controlling man, a demanding one, and boy, did it arouse her. She felt the cream drip from her cunt. His finger pressed lower, deeper down the crack of her ass to her cunt.

"Your body knows. Why fight it?" he asked and kissed her lips and then her cheek and chin, nibbling on the curve of it.

"Because things are weird. I don't know what you really think of me. I mean I told you I never sleep around, and that night with your brothers was so amazing, so different, and I was drunk, which is also something that never happens."

"I believe you. So do Pat and the others."

She shook her head. "I just feel so guilty about it all."

He pulled his fingers away from her pussy and ass and fixed her skirt. He pressed the material down and then placed a hand over her shoulder and one on her hip, caging her in against the wall.

She watched him pull his lower lip between his teeth as he stared into her eyes then lower, over her lips and breasts, then back up again.

"You shouldn't feel guilty because that night happened for a reason. It brought us together. Even meeting Pat and me the way you did was meant to be. Can't you just see it that way instead of analyzing it? We all make mistakes, but sometimes what we think might have been mistakes turn out to be choices, the right ones, and it all works out."

He cupped her cheek and his forearm leaned against her chest and shoulder. She reached up and held on to him. She stared up into his eyes. He was big and muscular, sexy, and smelled so good she inhaled just to keep smelling him and feeling his presence.

"I'm trying to."

He took a small breath and released it. "How about this? How about you just follow your heart, your body, and it will work out."

She gave a soft smile. "If I do that, then I'll be in your bed tonight."

He gave a soft smile, the first one she'd seen him give her, give anyone. He wrapped his arm around her waist and pulled her tightly as he pressed her back against the wall, pinning her there.

"Sounds like the perfect way to handle this." He suckled her neck, explored her skin with his mouth until she was tilting her head back and pushing her breasts up against his mouth. His tongue snuck into the cleavage of her breasts. Her pussy leaked and throbbed.

"Tobin, please. We should slow down. I don't want to screw this up."

He held her by her hips, and she pressed her hands to his chest as he looked into her eyes.

"You can't screw up something this perfect. Come on. Let's head back inside where I have backup to help get you to come home with us."

She tilted her head sideways at him, giving him a sassy look.

He pulled her closer as they began to walk, and then she felt the smack to her ass.

"Tobin."

"I know that turns you on. I can tell you're a naughty little thing. Come home with me tonight, and I guarantee you won't regret it."

Holy God, how can I say no to that?

* * * *

Pat watched Tobin return from the back hall with Brighid. She was hugging his arm, and he was walking like a man on a mission. Well, Pat was on a mission, too.

"There you are. We thought maybe you took off," Rusty teased her as he pulled her into his arms, hugged her close, and kissed her. His hand immediately went over her ass and squeezed for all to see. Brighid pressed her hands against Rusty's chest, and he released her lips.

"Rusty," she reprimanded. He held her gaze with a serious expression.

"I missed you, and this body," he said, and her cheeks turned a nice shade of red.

"I hope Tobin convinced you to come home with us when he had you all to himself," Reece said to her as he stepped closer and caressed her hair.

She lowered her eyes, and her cheeks turned a nice shade of red, and he thought she looked a bit intimidated.

"I'm still working on her. She has some reservations," Tobin said.

"I wonder what we can do to convince her. I mean I'm ready to get out the big guns if need be," Rusty said.

"Oh really? Like what?" she asked.

Pat placed the bottle of tequila down onto the bar right next to her. "Whatever it takes."

She gasped and placed her hands on her hips. "Really now?"

He started laughing and winked. But before she could say more, Jenny walked up to her in a hurry.

"I need the key to your place. We've got plans with these guys we met and are headed to another place."

Brighid blinked her eyes and looked a little shocked, and then her eyes went to her friends and a group of guys surrounding them. They looked to be having a good time, and her friends were feeling the alcohol they'd drunk.

"But I should come with you so I can help get you guys back to the condo."

"Are you kidding me? You stay here with the guys. Worry about you for once and what makes you happy. We'll be fine. Keys now please."

Pat watched Brighid reach into her small purse and pull out a keychain with a dragonfly charm on it attached to two keys. "Be careful," she said to Jenny.

"You be wild and go after what you deserve," Jenny said and hugged her. Then Jenny looked at Pat and the guys.

"You take care of my best girl or else." She then turned around and headed toward the group of friends and guys, who waved and said goodbye and headed out.

Pat pulled her toward him by wrapping her arm around her waist and pulling her back against his front. He kissed her neck and then whispered into her ear. "Sounds like we get to spend the rest of the night with you."

She held his gaze. "I want to do this right. That night with Reece and Rusty was amazing, but I did drink a lot, and if my head had been clear I probably wouldn't have done such a thing. The way all this is happening is just hard to process."

"Baby, what happened between us that night was meant to be," Rusty said. "The tequila, the good time, just made it easier to accept and not overanalyze it. Look how we found one another. We were looking for you, hoping to see you again. Every woman we would have met since we would have compared them to you."

Pat hugged her tight and kissed her cheek

Rusty ran his finger along her chin and pressed his hand against her lower back. "Come home with us because you feel what we feel."

She looked at Tobin then Reece and Pat.

"I was only teasing about the tequila," Pat said to her.

She tilted her head to the side so she could look at him. "Good, because this time I want to remember it all, and I expect breakfast in bed."

Pat felt like cheering aloud. Brighid was coming home with them to share, to make love together.

Rusty kissed the top of her head and squeezed her shoulders, and then he reached up and ran his pointer along her jaw, tilting her chin upward so he could lock gazes with her.

"Baby, you're going to be our breakfast in bed." He leaned closer and kissed her, and Pat looked at Tobin and Reece, who looked just as happy as Pat felt. Tonight was a big night. He and his brothers were about to claim their woman as theirs to share, and no other men would ever share her bed or get to touch her body but the McQuinn brothers.

* * * *

Brighid's heart was racing, her hands were sweating, and her body was so oversensitive even the feel of Pat's leg against her thigh was making her feel on fire. She didn't know how this was going to go down. As she started to wonder what would happen first, who would touch her first, undress her, and fuck her first, she became more aroused and needy.

They were all in the truck, and Tobin had just pulled onto the main road when Rusty turned in his seat.

"I need you so badly it aches," he said in a deep, rough voice that seemed to significantly affect her body. He grabbed her hips, lifted her up, shoved her skirt to her hips, and pulled her onto his lap. "Fuck slow. I need you."

She needed him, too, as she pressed her lips to his. She lifted up and felt his hard, large hands move along her bare thighs to her panties. She gripped onto his shoulders, ran her fingers through his hair, plunged her tongue into his mouth, savoring his taste, and then jerked as her panties were torn from her body.

A moment later, fingers thrust up into her cunt, and she widened her thighs and began to ride them. Pat was leaning in behind her, thrusting, stroking her cunt as Rusty unbuttoned her blouse. Pat's thick, hard fingers grazed the crack of her ass as he pulled them from her pussy and stroked over the sensitive spot. Then his fingers plunged back into her cunt as his teeth trailed along her back. Together, they undid the top and even her bra. Rusty released her lips and then pulled her clothing up over her head and tossed it to the side. He cupped her breasts.

"Holy fuck, baby, you're gorgeous. I love these big tits. I dreamt of them since our first night together." He opened his mouth, and she watched it descend onto her nipple and breast, where he suckled hard. Her body convulsed, and cream poured from her pussy.

"Fuck, yeah, she's coming, Rusty, all over my fucking fingers," Pat said, and Rusty pulled from her breast. Pat pulled his fingers out and trailed them over her ass. He applied a little pressure to her anus, and she gasped and rocked back.

"I need you now. Help me," he said to her.

She felt Pat's fingers leave her pussy, and then she began to undo Rusty's pants with him. As he pushed them down, he lifted his hips and shoved his pants from one leg. Pat pulled her to him and covered her mouth and kissed her deeply. His hand came around her side under her arm and cupped her breast. When he pulled back, he looked so carnal. He licked his fingers.

"You're fucking delicious."

He then pressed his fingers to her mouth. She didn't know how to react, but they had her feeling like some sexual goddess, so she played the part naturally. She held his gaze, slowly moved closer to his wet fingers, and licked her own cream from them.

Rusty grabbed her hips and lifted her up. He gave her a shake, and she focused on him.

"You're on the pill, right? I mean we didn't use any protection the first time and you're good, right?"

"Yes," she said, and he smiled.

He reached under her, aligned his cock with her pussy, and pushed her down as he thrust up.

"Oh." She gasped, tilted her head back, and felt his cock push deeper. He lifted her slightly and then shoved back up again until he fully penetrated her cunt.

"Fuck, I missed this pussy, this body. Fuck."

He grunted, and then they both began to fulfill their needs. With every thrust up and down, she felt her pussy tighten and Rusty's cock harden. Her breasts bounced up and down, and she used her thigh muscles to lift up and down along with his counter-thrusts. She wanted to feel more of his body and those sexy muscles. As he thrust upward, gripping her hips tightly, she lifted his shirt and pulled it up over his head.

He was so fine her heart skipped a beat. He had tattoos along his arms and one on his wrist. His pectoral muscles contracted and moved with each thrust he made.

"You're gorgeous," she said and lowered to lick his skin and then suckle his neck.

He squeezed her ass as he wrapped his arms around her, and they moved at record speed. He pressed her ass cheeks apart, and she felt the cool air against her overly warm body. Her anus clenched with need and the thought that she would have anal sex tonight aroused some deep inner need.

The truck stopped. She heard car doors open and close, and then he was lifting her up and placing her along the empty back seat. Pat had disappeared for a moment, and she looked for him, but Rusty began to thrust harder, faster into her.

He was relentless with his strokes. The leather in the back seat chafed her skin slightly, but she didn't care. Rusty had a thick, hard cock, and she was coming closer to orgasming once again.

He lifted her thigh higher. Her knee hit the leather seat, and she used it as leverage to get him to fuck her harder.

"Harder, Rusty. I'm almost there. I feel it."

He rocked faster, deeper. Her hair hung over the seat of the open passenger door. The cool evening air was a sharp contrast to her perspiring skin. She squeezed his arms, tilted her head back, and moaned.

"Rusty, oh God, Rusty, faster, I'm almost there."

He grunted and thrust, pulled her thighs tighter, his heavy body wedged between her legs so tightly she felt the deep pull, and he fucked her so hard she lost her breath as she came. He followed suit, moving in and out of her cunt and then holding his cock deeply in her as he sought his release then came inside of her. She could feel the cool caress of a breeze by the open side door, and there was Pat with his hands on his hips, smiling.

Rusty began kissing her throat, her breasts, and then her belly as he slid slowly out of her. He reached for his shirt and wiped between her legs with it.

"You are something else, Brighid. I'll never get enough of you." He kissed her deeply, and then he offered his hand to help her get up.

He had no qualms about standing in the driveway with only one leg in his pants around his ankle. She hadn't even realized they were at their place already.

But before she could feel out of sorts and shy, Pat was lifting her up into his arms and pulling her close, as if covering her body from anyone else's' view, and they all headed into their great big house.

* * * *

Pat's cock was so hard he was finding it painful to walk.

He somehow got Brighid up the stairs to the bedroom and set her feet down on the rug.

He took in the sight of her.

"You are a ten and then some, sweet baby. My God." He cupped her breast. He looked at them and absorbed how large, how plump and delicious they looked. Tobin moved in behind her, and as he unzipped her skirt, Pat feasted on her breasts. He licked one nipple and then the other. He suckled hard, and she moaned. Her skirt fell to the rug.

Pat felt her hands move along the waist of his jeans. She undid his button and zipper then shoved his pants down and stroked his cock.

He pulled from her breast. "God, your hands feel amazing. You're one sexy woman."

She smiled.

"That's a real sweet and feminine tattoo on your hip too, baby. I guess you have a thing for dragonflies?" Tobin asked as he lowered behind her and kissed along her tattoo.

Pat took her wrist and hand into his and brought her wrist to his lips.

"A really dainty one here, too. I like it." He licked along the tattoo on her wrist and then pulled her hand down over his cock. "Feel what you do to me? What watching you fuck my brother in the backseat of a truck has done to me, to us?"

She held his gaze with a very serious, aroused expression and gently massaged his cock and balls in her hand.

"I want to see all of you too," she said, and he took an unsteady breath, stepped his legs apart, and went to lift the hem of his shirt up to discard it as she shoved his pants down. Before he got it off, he felt her mouth on his cock, sucking him, licking him, and he tightened up, ready to come.

Her hot, wet mouth did a number to his cock in no time. He gripped her hair and rocked into her mouth until Tobin began to give orders.

"Reece, get the lube."

Brighid began to bend lower, and Pat moved onto the bed. She fell to her knees, spread his thighs, and then sucked on him faster.

Tobin caressed her back and played with her ass.

"I'm going to get this ass ready for my cock, baby. It's going to be nice and slick by the time we're ready to fuck you together. You be a good girl now and keep sucking Pat's cock," Tobin whispered against her ear and neck as he pressed against her back. Pat locked gazes with him, and Tobin winked.

But then she pushed her ass back, tapped Tobin's cock, and Tobin looked as though he was losing his mind.

"Fuck." He then widened her thighs and entered her pussy from behind in one quick stroke.

Pat felt his cock grow thicker and harder from her sucking him so hard at that moment. She drove them insane. He ran his hands along her shoulders and back. She was bent over him, sucking his cock and moving her hands up and down his thighs as Tobin stroked into her pussy from behind.

Tobin grabbed onto her shoulders and thrust his hips.

Pat sat there on the edge of the bed as she worked his cock and Tobin grunted and moaned. Then he saw Reece standing there with the tube of lube, smacking it against the palm of his hand and waiting for his turn.

Smack, smack, smack.

The feel of her jerking and moaning while Turbo fucked her pussy and smacked her ass was making it hard to hold back and not come. But he wanted to be inside her pussy when he came just as it seemed Tobin wanted.

"God damn, she's so tight. Fuck I'm there. I'm there, Brighid. Come for me," Tobin demanded. He pulled her hands behind her back, causing her shoulders to hit Pat's thighs as she continued to suck him down.

He saw the sexy tattoo on her wrist, and the way Tobin restrained her had them all complimenting the scene.

"Fuck, she likes being restrained. Holy fucking shit, she looks sexy, like our own little sex goddess," Reece said.

Tobin stroked her relentlessly, and then Pat felt her shake as if she was coming just as Tobin grunted aloud that he was coming as he shot his seed into her pussy.

They were all breathing heavy, but Pat was feeling crazy, as if he could lose his mind if he didn't come soon.

He gripped her hair just as Reece lowered to his knees and squirted lube to her ass.

She gasped and lifted up, and Pat pulled her higher.

"Fuck me while Reece gets that ass ready for his cock. Come on now, baby. You need to take us all together," he said to her, and he saw Rusty return from the bathroom with a towel and wash his cock off. Brighid lowered over Pat's cock and began to ride him.

"Oh God, that feels so weird, Reece. You're so hard, Pat." She continued to rock slowly on his cock. Pat could see Brighid's eyes widen, and then an aroused expression filled her face. He knew that Reece was getting her prepared for them. "How does that feel, baby? Are you ready for all of us? He felt the pressure against his cock.

"Yes. Oh God, yes."

"I won't last long, bud. You need to fuck that ass now," Pat told Reece.

"Oh Please. Please, Reece, more," she begged and rocked her hips as she lay her cheek against Pat's chest. Her ass was lifted slightly, and then Pat heard the smacks to her ass. She moaned and then cried out again.

"Oh God."

Reece replaced his fingers with his cock and stroked right into her ass.

* * * *

Back and forth he moved deeper and deeper until she felt an odd sensation and a sense of relief. Two cocks were inside of her at once. Then she felt the fingers under her chin, and Rusty was there with his cock in his hand, stroking it.

She knew what he wanted, but she closed her eyes and relished the feel of both Reece and Pat fucking her.

"So fucking good. God damn, baby, I love this ass. I love sharing you with my brothers like this. You're so fucking incredible," Reece told her, and she lifted up, felt the desire to please them, and opened her mouth and accepted Rusty's cock. She was breathing deeply, the sensations overwhelming as Rusty's scent filled her nostrils while Pat's cock fucked her pussy and Reece fucked her ass. She'd never had anal sex before, and thank God, she liked it. It felt so naughty, so sensual and right.

Smack, smack, smack.

Reece spanked her, and then she heard him grunt and felt his cock thicken as he came and cried out her name.

Pat followed, and she remained in position, sucking on Rusty until Pat finished releasing his seed.

"Here we go, baby," Tobin said. His arm wrapped around her waist from behind once Reece pulled from her ass.

Rusty pulled his cock from her mouth, and she gasped for air. Pat got out from under her.

Rusty took his place, and Tobin placed her right back on top of Rusty, where she immediately sank down onto his shaft. They both moaned and then began to stroke and thrust, trying to find their rhythm. She felt so sensitive. Even the feel of her inner thighs hitting Rusty's hard thighs as she sank down onto his cock touched her to her core.

She never felt so desirable and so turned on in her entire life. It was almost magical, life altering, and she wanted more of it. She gripped his shoulders and counterthrust against him. She felt wild, needy, yet her pussy didn't stop coming and exploding. She was so wet she felt it soaking between her and Rusty, who was pulling her down for a kiss. Even the way his large, hard hand gripped her hair and tugged her lower made her come more. He plunged his tongue in deeply, and she kissed him back as they battled for control of that kiss.

She felt the cool liquid and then her ass cheeks being spread right before Tobin's cock began to push into her ass.

She wanted it, felt the need to become one with them, and this was a hell of a way to do it.

A moment later, after several small strokes, he was balls deep in her ass and he and Rusty were fucking her together.

She tried joining in and lifting up, but they were so big, so muscular and in control that she felt wild and uncoordinated. Her body rocked and swayed. Her breasts felt so tender, and every shake aroused her more and more, and she cried out another release. Rusty grunted and then came, and then Tobin followed.

"Brighid! Oh Brighid." Tobin grunted in a deep, loud voice and then massaged her ass cheeks and ran his hands up and down her back as she collapsed against Rusty's chest.

Tobin's hands massaged her muscles and made her shiver and shake in the aftereffects of their lovemaking. It was crazy, wild, and she felt her energy drain as she lay against Rusty.

They were all breathing rapidly, and then Tobin pulled slowly from her ass and Rusty rolled her to her side. Reece was there with a warm washcloth and towel, and Pat climbed up next to her and kissed her forehead. She looked at all four of them. They were staring at her, smiling.

"Baby, you set this place on fire. Damn." Tobin ran his hands up and down her thigh.

She closed her eyes and relished their touches. She'd never felt so safe, so content, as though she belonged. Suddenly she prayed these men didn't break her heart and leave her now that they'd had her. She was glad her eyes were closed. She couldn't understand the sudden fear of abandonment, of rejection, and she began to sit up. She reached for something to cover herself with, but she couldn't. The sheets and comforter were below them.

"Slow down, doll, you shouldn't get up so quickly," Pat said to her.

Rusty cupped her cheeks and rolled her to her back, straddling her body so she couldn't move.

"Don't even think of trying to run off. This is special. This is perfect. We want you in our lives. No regrets, only more days and nights like this one. You got it?" he said very seriously, and she couldn't help but get teary-eyed.

"I'm going to be honest here and tell you that I'm freaking out a little. This whole situation, the circumstances around us meeting and having tonight, isn't what I expected."

He smiled and then looked at his brothers then at her. He cupped her breast.

"Sweetie, this isn't like any of us would have ever expected, but that's why it's so incredible. Now enough serious talk. It's bad enough I'm feeling this damn possessive of you. We all have things to work out, but know this isn't a one-night stand. Not for us anyway."

"Not for me either," she admitted then laid back and closed her eyes as Rusty continued to explore her breasts with his mouth and Pat leaned over and kissed her.

Chapter 4

Brighid stepped out of the shower to find Reece there holding a towel for her. She stepped into it, and he wrapped her up in the fluffy material and then lifted her into his arms. She was surprised but also very aroused again. His dark hair was wet from his shower, his muscles huge with veins, and cords of other muscles everywhere. She had never seen so much perfect male physique in one place before. All four men were in excellent physical condition.

She wrapped her arms around his shoulders and neck as best she could, but he had her to the bed in no time.

He laid her on it and then leaned on his side and elbow and stared down into her eyes. She didn't move a muscle. She couldn't. He was just so beautiful.

"I don't want you to think I'm crazy, baby, but I don't like you out of my sight." He slowly began to pull the towel away from her body. She felt like a gift being unwrapped as his eyes looked over her breasts and then her pussy.

She held his gaze. Those dark blue eyes affected her in so many ways.

"I'm not going anywhere, Reece." She shivered as he dragged his pointer along her skin softly, sensually roaming over her nipple then her ribs and belly to her pussy.

"I guess it's because of that night in the hotel and how Rusty and I woke up to find you gone. I didn't like it." He gently pinched her nipple and tugged. Her lips parted.

She could overanalyze his remarks and feelings, or she could take them as another sign that he had been just as affected from their connection that night as she was. She was starting to believe that he and his brothers were meant to be hers. The last thing she wanted to do was hurt Reece or the others.

"Will it help if I say I'm sorry, that I panicked?" she asked him and stared into his eyes deeply, feeling so flirty and sexy it was amazing and empowering.

"I think you can make it up to me, to us." He tugged on her nipple again. She felt the imaginary line from her nipple to her pussy, and then cream dripped from deep within. She wanted to please him, them, and make it up to him so he and Rusty would know she wanted this to work out.

"Anything you want."

His eyes widened slightly, and he leaned over and licked her left nipple. "Anything?" Those damn dark blue eyes were so sexy, and that grin, the mischievous expression, was to die for.

"Hmmm, why do I get the feeling that you're going to test my limits?"

He smirked as he lowered his mouth to her breast and suckled. She closed her eyes, and then he released it with a pop. "It's interesting that you say test your limits because, you see, you, and this incredibly sexy body, have started quite the fire burning in me and my brothers. Never, and I mean never, has a woman made my dick so hard and made me want so much, desire every ounce of her in every way, like I do you. I feel possessive, needy, hungry, Brighid. I've got lots of fantasies twirling around in my head."

He pinched her nipple and then trailed his fingers down her belly to her pussy. He stroked her clit with his thumb and forefinger.

Her lips parted as she continued to hold his gaze and feel, anticipating his fingers stroking her and bringing her to climax. In a flash, she imagined his mouth on her, his tongue plunging deeply and then his fingers stroking her anus. She tightened her ass.

"This is what I want from you right now." He slowly stuck the tip of his finger up into her cunt. He used his thumb to tease her clit. She was wet, and he knew he'd done that to her.

"To do as I ask. No questions, no resisting. I want you to give me complete control of your body. Whatever I ask of you, you'll do because you trust me and my brothers and you believe that what we started is real."

He stroked her pussy and then pulled his fingers from her cunt and brought them to her lips.

"Taste your sweet cream, baby."

Her heart hammered. He was so wild, sexy, commanding, and she hadn't realized how turned on the idea of giving him complete control over her would make her feel.

She opened her mouth slowly and licked his finger. He pushed it a little deeper, and she sucked it just like she would suck his cock.

"Good girl, Brighid. See how delicious you taste? I'm going to feast on that sweet fucking cunt while I explore your ass and get you ready for my brothers and me again. How does that sound?"

"Amazing," she whispered, feeling almost drugged by his touch, his words, and what was yet to come. The anticipation was arousing in itself.

He sat up and pulled off his pants. She saw his long, thick cock lift up and tap against his belly. She licked her lips.

He pressed over her, and his cock tapped against her pussy lips, and she nearly moaned. She felt his hands massage from her hands over her wrists and then move them up over her head. His heavy, muscular thighs caressed against her inner thighs, and her pussy leaked more cream.

Reece held her gaze. He tapped her arms.

"Don't move them," he warned.

His expression and the tone of his voice, so deep, sensual, and rough, melted over her skin and penetrated to her soul. She was aroused and needy, and he knew it.

He lifted up. She felt his palm press against her calf and then slowly move along the curve of her leg.

"Open for me."

"For us," Rusty chimed in, joining them.

She jerked, surprised at the other male voice, but smiled at Rusty. He winked at her as he strolled in naked, hair wet from probably a shower and looking ready to fill her up with his thick, long cock, too.

More cream dripped from her pussy as Rusty lowered to his knees on the floor by the edge of the bed. He and Reece ran their hands up her inner calf to her thighs. She shook and shivered. Her natural response was to close her legs, but they wouldn't let her.

Both men held her thighs wider and locked onto her eyes.

"Don't close them. Give us complete control, and we promise that it will be well worth it," Rusty said to her as he leaned forward and kissed her inner thigh.

Reece did the same thing on her other side, both making their way higher.

Her breasts felt so needy they tingled and throbbed, waiting to be touched. She began to move a little, and Reece gripped her hipbone. "Lie still and feel."

Then she felt the tongue against her clit before it lashed out at her pussy lips.

"Rusty." She moaned and shook her head side to side.

She felt the hands move under her ass and pull her farther off the bed. Reece latched onto her breast and began to feast on it. She shivered and moaned when Rusty licked from her cunt to her anus. Back and forth, back and forth. She felt the tightness in her core. Then he lifted up and slid his cock back and forth over her pussy then to her anus.

She could hardly take it.

"Please. Oh God, that feels so good." She moved her hands. Reece gripped them.

"Keep them up there. Hand over all control and don't hold back."

She raised them back up, widened her thighs, and relished the feel of Rusty's cock sliding back and forth over her pussy and ass.

Then he pulled back and pressed his fingers to her cunt.

"So sweet and wet for us. I think our girl needs a cock in her." he teased and pressed his fingers to her cunt. She felt her pussy muscles grip his digit tightly, and he moved it in and out of her. Her core tightened and cramped with the need to come.

"Please, Rusty. Oh!" She gasped as Reece pulled on her nipple and then suckled more of her breast into his mouth.

A moment later she felt Rusty bend down, and then she felt the cool liquid against her anus, but as she got used to the idea that he was about to take her there, Rusty shocked her as the tip of his cock pressed against her pussy lips and then shoved in deeply.

"Oh!" She exhaled, and Rusty began a series of strokes that seemed to be affecting him. His expression was tense, his teeth clenched. He gripped her hips and began to sink in and out faster, deeper. His eyes locked onto her breasts as they bounced up and down and made her feel sexy and wild.

"I'm ready," Reece said, and she looked at him lying beside her with his cock in his hand, stroking it.

"Well, look at this," Tobin said joining them in the bedroom, along with Pat.

It made her pussy quake, and she came. "Oh." She moaned.

Rusty pulled out and then lifted her up into his arms and kissed her deeply. She ran her fingers through his hair and kissed him back until she felt the finger stroke along the crack of her ass.

"I need some of that too," Tobin said, and Rusty pulled from her lips, turned her around, and placed her on top of Reece.

Reece aligned his cock with her pussy, and Brighid sank right down onto his shaft and exhaled.

Reece gripped her wrists and brought them above his head and over the mattress causing her to fall forward, her breasts to his chest. Hands pressed her thighs apart, and she knew it was Rusty as Reece thrust upward. In this position she could hardly move to ride him. Reece kept her arms gripped above him, and he would thrust upward and then hold himself deep before pulling back down.

"I love this ass, baby. I love playing with it," Rusty said and ran his hands along both globes. "I love spanking it."

Smack, smack.

"And I love fucking it." He then pressed the lubricant into her ass with his fingers.

"Oh God, it's too much," she said with her arms still above restrained above Reece's head, her breasts now in his face as he licked and suckled her breasts while Rusty fingered her ass. She started moving her hips, and then Rusty pulled his fingers from her ass.

"Here I come, baby, and get that mouth ready for cock, too." He then slowly pressed his cock to her anus and slid right in. She felt the fullness. She exhaled with relief, and so did the others.

"Sweet mother, she's so fucking tight. I love this. This feels so good, so right," Reece told her as he gripped her ass cheeks, squeezed them, pinched them, and then massaged them. He and Rusty began to move when Pat joined them, taking a fistful of her hair to get her attention and bringing her lips closer to his cock.

She felt wild, uninhibited, aroused, and wanton as she opened for him and immediately sucked on Pat's cock.

"That's right, baby, take it all in. Get as much as you can in there. We're going to come inside every hole and make you all ours officially," Pat told her.

Smack.

She mumbled against Pat's cock as Tobin joined in and began to spank her ass.

In a flash, Reece, Rusty, and Pat began to move in sync, and she couldn't even assist. She just kept sucking Pat's cock until Rusty grunted and came. She licked and sucked Pat, and then he growled low and shot his seed down her throat. She suckled and licked him clean. and then he sat back moaning, and he and Rusty grinned.

Smack, smack.

"I love seeing this ass nice and pink while I fuck it good," Tobin said. She felt the cool liquid and, a moment later, his cock pressing against her anus.

"Oh God. Oh." She moaned, and he slid into her ass. When he was fully seated inside of her, he and Reece began a series of faster, deeper strokes. She was panting as Reece placed her hands back over his head, causing her breasts to reach his lips and her ass to stick out farther as her legs spread wider.

Smack, smack, smack.

She grunted and felt her core tighten. They were relentless as they both fucked her hard until she cried out as she came, and then Reece and Tobin followed.

"Holy Jesus, baby, you're amazing. That was fucking amazing." Tobin massaged her ass as he slid his cock out and then bent over to kiss her shoulders, her back, and then her ass. He gave a light tap before he disappeared into the other room.

Reece cupped her cheeks and held her gaze as he stared up into her eyes.

"You're all ours now, Brighid. No turning back now. This can only get better," Reece said and kissed her.

She hugged him tightly and kissed him thoroughly until he slid his cock from her pussy, rolled her to her side, and then kept her close in his arms, a place she definitely could get used to being.

Chapter 5

Stark shook his head in an attempt to focus on the task at hand. But he couldn't. His blood boiled with anger, hatred toward Brighid and the four men she'd gone home with last night. The fucking whore. *She'll pay for it. She'll suffer and so will those men.* Two of the fuckers worked for two local firehouses. Both just so happened to be here in town, near the street he needed to do this job on. It was meant to be. For them to die fighting the flames. He'd pick them off one by one if need be. He'd talk to Brighid. Get to know her. Befriend her as she mourned the loss of her new lovers.

His stomach ached something terrible as he placed the chemical mixture along the outside of the boiler system. It was an old one, getting ready to go. He could see the small leak already emitting discharge from the base. This place was going to go up in flames sooner rather than later, but he wouldn't stop what he was doing. He was getting paid for this, and that meant money in his pocket for him to disappear with Brighid.

He began to pour the chemicals in a thin line along the base and down the side wall. Right above from the basement was a fireplace. a gas one. As the flames ignited and the walls burst into orange, red, and black, they would penetrate the flooring, go straight up to the first floor from the basement, and blow sky high, but not until just about that moment when the firefighters arrived. Hopefully both of the ones he wanted dead.

He spilled the chemicals a little too much and cursed at his mistake. There was nothing to wipe it up with, but that didn't matter. None of the previous fires exposed the accelerant, a concoction he created himself. He would get away with this, and he would get away with taking Brighid, his angel of fire, and disappear.

* * * *

"Monday's suck," Brighid said when she got into the office early to start working on more files. It had been a hell of a weekend, and that brought a smile to her face and brightness to her heart. She hadn't wanted it to end and neither had the guys, but they all had work this morning, and she needed to get back to her place to say goodbye to her friends before they left.

She missed the guys. That was crazy, but even thinking about them made her aroused and ready for their embraces, their kisses, and even their cocks.

She chuckled as she took a sip of her coffee and nearly spilled some from her lips. She couldn't wait to see them again. They were perfect in every aspect of the word. Her friends carried on about how lucky she was and how thrilled they were to finally see her happy. She was happy. She felt as if everything in her life was finally falling into place.

As she logged into her computer, she saw the little box pop up indicating the time and date of her last log-in. Normally she wouldn't even pay attention to it, but the date and the time was not correct. She wouldn't be here at one o'clock in the morning to log in. She felt that uneasy feeling in her gut. Could someone have known her password and gone in there? The only ones who knew her password were Lenny and Ray, but why would they go in there?

She scrolled into the systems files and, after a bit of clicking, came across the most recent changes to the system. A file for accounting, billing, and a specific account came up. Bricker Daily? That was the man who'd showed up Friday right before she left. He handed her a check for a full year's payment and said that Lenny told him to drop it off. That he was a friend.

She scrolled down with her mouse and started clicking on screens. A client since when? she wondered. She took great pride in knowing every account and client. She had a system of remembering them and associating them with different things. Her photographic memory was an added bonus and an asset she didn't tell people about. Names, faces, lots of useless information was stored in her little brain computer inside her head, and she was able to reference things sometimes word for word after reading about it once. It was a gift and a burden in the same.

She looked through the files and noted a series of yearly checks, insurance payments that were added in all in the same log-in time frame. Someone had added these to the account. Friday, when he'd dropped off the check right before she was leaving, she'd handed it to accounting for them to process the payment and update the account. She was so busy trying to finish things up and get home to meet her friends that she hadn't really thought about not knowing this Bricker client. Something wasn't right. That thought had her thinking about her bosses' odd behavior lately. She'd thought maybe they were growing too large, too soon, but this was more than that.

"Good morning, Brighid."

She jumped at the sound of Lenny's voice as he came out of the office smiling. He placed a few folders down on her desk.

"You look beautiful this morning. Did you have a nice weekend?" he asked, smiling as he looked her over.

"Oh, yes, it was great."

"Your friends enjoy visiting the town?" he asked, and she remembered telling him and Ray about it Friday morning because she had planned to leave thirty minutes earlier than usual.

"Yes, they loved it." She wondered if she should ask him about the files. She didn't like people logging into her computer system. It made her feel violated, as if she didn't have control over her responsibilities and anything could go wrong. Maybe she should just change the password and then wait for them to notice, and when they asked her, she could say that she'd seen some glitches in the system and was afraid someone could hack in, so every so often, she would change the password. Or she could just come straight out and accuse him of logging in without her permission. But he was the boss. God, she hated confrontations.

"I placed these files here because they're new clients to be added to the system. If you could do that for me and then send the information to accounting?"

"Sure. Oh, and I took the check that Bricker Daily gave me Friday and sent it along to accounting."

Lenny's eyes widened. A flash of something went across his face and eyes, but he quickly recovered and gave a nod.

"Great. He said he would stop by instead of mailing it. I haven't seen him in such a long time." He then looked around them before looking back at her.

"I never heard of him before. Didn't even know he was a client."

Lenny looked at her and suddenly seemed very serious. Her gut clenched.

"He's been a client for several years. Just like a lot of other people this way. It was part of why we wanted to get a more central location to the business. Well, I need to get moving on some work. Glad you had a good weekend."

He walked away. Could she have possibly missed the account somehow? she wondered, but she knew that wasn't the case. She was pretty damn anal about things. What if he was doing something illegal? No. No, he couldn't be. Why was she thinking this? Why was she being suspicious? God, one night with a detective and a cop, and she thought she was Dick fucking Tracy.

She took a deep breath and released it as she stared at the screen. Her mind and her suspicion got the best of her as she began to take screen shots of the items and the log-in times. Just in case something was wrong, she wouldn't get blamed for it. She then went and changed the password and took a screen shot of the time and day she did so. She took those screen shots and added them to a private secure file. Maybe she watched too many mystery movies, but if not, then she had proof she wasn't responsible.

She went back to doing her work, never really losing the uneasy feeling until her cell phone went off. She glanced down and saw the text from Reece.

Miss you already, beautiful. Looking forward to tonight.

She couldn't help but to smile and then respond.

Miss you, too. Have a good day at work. Be safe.

She sent the message without even thinking first. She was dating two firefighters and two law enforcement officers. They had dangerous jobs. How the hell was she going to not panic and worry about them all the time? That anxious, uneasy feeling hit her gut. She was not prepared for this. Not prepared for a ménage relationship with four individually demanding, large, strong-minded men. Not prepared for the worry, the uneasy feelings that something could happen to any of them at any given time. Jesus. *I can feel my heart racing.*

She covered her hand over her heart and felt the pounding. She then felt that queasy unease rattling in her gut and chest. Was she having an anxiety attack over this?

Always, sweetheart. Gotta go.

He texted back, and she swallowed hard. The sound of a fire whistle going off in the distance added to her fears. Holy crap. Was she just texting Reece when they got a fire call? *He's leaving for it now maybe?* she wondered, and a few moments later the deep, loud honking of fire engines went passing by the front of the office. She stood up and saw the men in the truck as it whizzed by.

Keep Reece and the others safe, God. Please.

* * * *

"Officer McQuinn. Got smoke and individuals inside of The Boardwalk gift shop off of Luana Highway. Getting people out now. Need fire department dispatched. Over."

Pat was filtering through the main floor and getting people out of there. He'd just happened to stop his patrol car across the way to get a coffee at the bake shop when he saw the smoke and people pointing. He ran across the street as he called it in. As he helped an elderly couple out of the building, along with the owner, he heard the explosion and covered the elderly couple as they fell to the sidewalk. Debris hit them instantly, but he felt as if he'd taken the brunt of it. He couldn't hear a thing. It was as though the shock of the explosion had damaged his eardrums. But then he heard the large honking of fire engines. He checked the elderly couple.

"Are you okay?" he asked them, but as he moved, he felt the aches to his back and his legs.

"Yes, yes, I think so," the older man said, and then they started getting up as firefighters began pulling out the hose and another started spraying into the fire. It was very hot where they were.

"You're hurt. Oh God," the older lady said, and when he went to move, he felt the pinch to his side.

"Jesus, Pat, you're fucking bleeding and covered with glass and debris," Reece yelled out and knelt down, placing his hand on his shoulder. "Don't move. The paramedics are just pulling up."

"Shit, I'm fine. I just can't fucking hear shit," he said, and when he moved his arm, he felt the pain. Other firefighters were preparing to enter the building.

"I need to go. You're sure you're okay?" Reece asked, not wanting to leave him.

"Yeah, yeah, go do your fucking job," Pat said, and Reece gave a wink and then stood up.

Pat could hear his chief giving orders as Mercury approached with other paramedics. It was total chaos. The sound of other engine companies could be heard in the distance as they approached. It was probably his brother Rusty's Company 20 coming to help Ladder Company 18.

"Lie still. You've got shit sticking out of your arms, shoulder, and legs," Mercury told him.

"I can't hear shit. There was a huge fucking explosion as I just got this couple out of the building," Pat told Mercury and the other paramedics.

"He saved us. We could have all been killed, but he got everyone out of there," the older man said, and then another explosion happened with more screaming as they covered their heads, but nothing fell over them. This time it was inside the building where the firefighters were.

"Fuck, Reece is in there," Pat yelled as Mercury stood up and looked back across the way.

"It looks like it happened farther back. They had just gone through the front entrance. Now the two bordering storefronts are smoking. It's a fucking mess," Mercury said to him.

"Did they get everyone out?" Pat asked.

"Everyone's out," one of the other firefighters told them. "But we've got no response from five of our firemen inside the building."

"What? Oh God, Reece, Rusty and the others? Who's in there with them?" Pat asked as he painstakingly stood up on his knees. He felt the pinching, and sure enough, he had glass sticking out of his pants.

"Pat, lie still. We don't know how deep those shards of glass are imbedded in your skin. You need to go to the hospital," Mercury said as he gripped Pat's shoulder.

"What the hell is going on? Shit, Pat, are you okay?"

Pat heard Tobin's voice as he approached and looked frantic. He bent down next to him.

"He needs to lie down and be still so we can get him on the gurney and take him to the hospital. We don't know how deep the wounds are," Mercury told Tobin.

"I'm fine. I'm not going anywhere until I know Reece and Rusty and the others are okay."

"Reece and Rusty are in there?" Tobin asked.

"It's a fucking mess," one of the firefighters said, and Tobin stood up.

"I'll find the chief and get an update," Tobin said. "Pat, you need medical attention. I've got a patrol officer by your vehicle, but it's all covered in shit, and the glass is broken. Take care of him, Mercury." Tobin then walked over toward the fire trucks.

* * * *

"Son of a bitch. What the fuck was that?" Reece asked as the explosion rocked the building, taking out the entire back entrance from the basement to the first floor. He couldn't believe they were alive and not buried in concrete and wood.

"Reece?"

Reece heard the yelling and then turned to see another firefighter, and he recognized the colored stripe down the side. Ladder 20. Reece was pulling shit off of Corporal and Steve, two firefighters in his company. Brandon Polaski and Jenks St. James came up through the dust and debris, spraying down the fire that was burning in the corner of the room near them, along with Rusty.

"Are you okay?" Rusty asked them as they helped Reece, Corporal, and Steve get up. Steve was limping, and Reece felt his arm throbbing something terrible.

"A bit banged up but fucking alive. We need to get the fuck out of here. This isn't right. Two fucking explosions," Reece said to him.

Rusty placed his hand on his shoulder. "You guys head out to the paramedics. We've got more men coming in now and around the back, too." Rusty heard creaking, and everyone stood still.

"Everyone out!" Rusty yelled, and they dropped the line, and they all ran from the storefront. Rusty grabbed onto Reece, and they were the last ones to exit the doorway when the building began to slowly collapse from the back roof to the front. They all tumbled into the roadway as the sky and area around them filled with gray smoke and debris. It was a fucking mess and a half, and definitely suspicious if Reece knew anything about fire.

* * * *

Everyone was talking about the huge fire and the explosions that rocked even their building more than two blocks away. As they headed outside of the insurance office to see, they kept their distance and prayed that everyone was okay. Brighid felt her heart pounding as she worried about the first responders and any customers who could have been in the storefront. Little bits of information, gossip, or hearsay filtered through the crowd of people. They said multiple police and firefighters had been injured and that the building had collapsed and now they were trying to control the damage and fire so the adjacent storefronts wouldn't go up in flames, too.

After a while, as she kept glancing at her phone, she saw and heard a series of ambulances go by in the direction of the hospital. She was sick with worry as the office staff headed back inside. When she sat down at her desk, she couldn't concentrate. She tried being rational and telling herself that she couldn't react this way every time there was a fire. She would be a constant nervous wreck, and it could piss off her men and make her annoying.

But then her cell phone rang. She saw that it was Tobin.

"Hello?" When she answered it, she heard how frantic her voice sounded and how loud she had answered. Everyone in the office nearby looked at her.

"Brighid, there's a bad fire going on a few blocks from your office."

"I know. We heard the firetrucks and then explosions. Is everyone okay? What the hell is going on?"

Now the rest of the staff was walking closer. She looked at them and felt the tears in her eyes. It was as if she knew something was wrong.

"Pat was the first on the scene as he was patrolling by. He got people out, but the first explosion went off, and he got hurt."

"No. Oh God, is he okay?" she asked, gripping the phone tighter.

"He's at the hospital and so are Reece and Rusty, plus about five other firefighters. It's a mess."

"Reece and Rusty got hurt too? How badly?"

"They're okay, Brighid. Just some debris and glass. Pat is cut up a bit, and they need to be careful removing the shards of glass. Reece hurt his arm, and Rusty banged up his knee and leg as they evaded the collapse."

"The building nearly collapsed on them? Oh God. What can I do? What do you need from me? Should I go to the hospital?"

"Sweetie, they're okay. You can head there. I need to stay on scene."

"Is it safe, Tobin? I don't want you getting hurt, too. This is scary enough."

"Brighid, it's our jobs, baby. I need to go. It's a fucking mess."

"Okay. Be careful. I'll go to the hospital now."

She disconnected the call.

"Brighid, who was that?" Ray asked her as he joined the other staff near her desk.

"My friends were hurt in the fire and explosion. I need to go to the hospital." She felt numb and shaking, and as she grabbed her bag, she knocked over her files.

Ray gently took her arm. "I'll drive you. You're shaking and could have an accident getting there. Come on."

They all told her they hoped her friends were okay. Before she walked out the door, saying thank you, she spotted Lenny by the front desk. He looked concerned to say the least, and her gut clenched again, but then Ray was pulling her along with him as he opened the front door and they headed out.

* * * *

"Come here, baby," Rusty said to Brighid as she stood by the doorway afraid to come any closer, arms crossed and looking so fragile and scared. There was a gash to his arm that needed stitches, and they were waiting to hear about Pat and Reece. The nurse gave her a smile.

"You can come sit right next to him. I'll go check on your brothers, Rusty," the nurse, Catalina, told him as Brighid walked closer.

Rusty pulled her onto his lap instead of onto the chair. When she wrapped her arms around his neck and hugged him, he knew she had been so scared. He had been worried, too. About Pat and Reece and the others. The scent of her shampoo and the feel of her feminine body in his arms and on his lap eased his worry. She healed him, made him feel whole, good, and lucky to have found her. He kissed her neck and chin.

"It's okay, sweetheart. I'm fine. It's just a cut."

She pulled back, and he could see the tears in her eyes.

"You needed fifteen stitches. That's not nothing," she scolded him. He raised one of his eyebrows at her, and she immediately blushed and lowered her eyes. His dick got instantly hard.

"I'm sorry. I was scared from the moment I heard the firetrucks and sirens go by the office. Well, even before that, I was thinking about you and the guys and worrying about your professions. I'm not used to this. To feeling so close to anyone and worrying. I've been on my own for a while now. I mean I have my friends, but this is different."

He chuckled and kissed her chin.

"Baby, of course it is because of what we shared over the weekend. You're part of us, and we're part of you. Making love was special, and the bond is deep and strong."

He caressed her hair and her cheek as she held his gaze with those gorgeous green eyes of hers. He squeezed her hip, loving the sexy business dress in small black and white polka dots she wore today. When she'd walked into the emergency room, wearing those high heels and looking so sexy and sophisticated, catching everyone's attention, he'd been jealous and proud. His buddies left them alone to go check on Reece, Rusty, and the others.

She hugged him again and then stood up and pressed her hands down the material of the dress.

"How long before I can check on Reece and Pat?" she asked.

"Reece is in x-ray, and Pat is right next door, giving everyone hell. Perhaps the two of you could go in and calm him a bit?" Catalina said to them as she came back into the room.

Rusty stood up and took Brighid's hand.

"Come on, baby, sounds like Pat is being a baby," he teased.

"You said x-rays for Reece? Why?" Brighid asked.

"He injured his arm, and it's all bruised up and swollen. The doctor wants to make sure there's no fractures. He isn't too happy either, but he's cooperating," Catalina told them.

As they entered the other room and saw the doctor shaking his head, Rusty knew that Pat was being resistant.

"Well, Mr. Uncooperative, I have some visitors that may make you a bit calmer about this situation," Catalina said and then motioned for Brighid to come closer.

Pat was lying on the table, his pants cut up and blood oozing along the bit of skin. He had shards of glass sticking out of him in different spots.

"Jesus, Pat, you look like a fucking porcupine," Rusty teased, and Brighid let go of his hand and went around the front of the table.

"Fuck you, Rusty," he barked. "Heard you needed stiches. Pansy."

"Pat," Brighid scolded, and Pat turned to look.

"Brighid?" he whispered, and to Rusty's ears, it sounded like shock and thrill in his brother's voice.

"We need to cut his pants and get a clearer view of the damage to make sure nothing is too deep or in need of stitches," the doctor said.

Brighid leaned over in front of Pat. She clutched his cheeks between her hands.

"I was so worried. Let them work so I know that you're okay."

"I'm not okay with a bunch of fucking people looking at my naked body while I lie here helpless."

"You can keep the underwear on. There's nothing on your backside," the doctor said to him.

"Come on, Pat, and do it. I'm worried." She then kissed him.

Rusty smirked.

"Fine, do it and get this shit over with. I said I'm fine," Pat barked. But a few minutes later, after the uniform pants were cut from his body and the view of the shards of glass were clearer, even Rusty cringed.

Son of a bitch, that looks like it hurts like hell.

* * * *

Pat tried focusing on Brighid's green eyes and not the sharp pain he felt as the doctor began to slowly take out the shards of glass. The doctor would warn him when the deeper ones were being pulled. He needed a few stitches here and there to keep the skin closed to heal better. But they were the kind that would disintegrate as the cuts healed, so they weren't so bad. By the time the doctor was finished, Pat felt exhausted. He was trying so hard to not show pain and keep a smile on his face because Brighid looked about ready to cry. It was an odd sensation to have these feelings, to have a woman, their woman, by their side like this when they got injured on the job. He'd bet she was scared now about their professions. He hoped it didn't make her want to pull back and out some distance between them. They would have to talk about it together and help her to deal with being a first responder's woman.

"That slit at the top of your dress is pretty low cut for work. Can't you button it up more?" he asked her.

She looked him in the eyes and shook her head.

"It's not too low cut, and no, this is the way it's made." She ran her thumbs along his jaw and then pressed her lips to his. "I'm so glad that you're not hurt worse. I heard you rescued a bunch of people and took the brunt of the hit to protect an elderly couple."

"Don't tell him about the local news crews waiting to interview him. It will go to his head," Rusty said aloud.

Catalina chuckled. "It's honorable what he did. Saving all those people who could have gotten caught inside the burning building. That cute elderly couple has been talking non-stop about him and how he covered them to protect them."

"Well, it's better than them suing me for bruising them up as I tackled them to the ground," Pat added.

"You're not kidding," Rusty said.

"People do that kind of thing?" Brighid asked, sounding so sweet and innocent. He loved that about her. She seemed untouched by violence or the cruel intentions of evil people.

"They sure do. There's a lot of bad out there," Rusty added.

"Well, I'd like to think there are more good people than bad people like that. I'm just glad that you guys are all okay."

Pat gave her a soft smile. She really was so sweet and untainted by the negatives in society. Perhaps that was why he and his brothers were so into her. They each dealt with negativity on a daily basis. They saw a lot of bad, evil, and criminal things in their line of work, especially Tobin. She represented a positive, a light in the darkness that showed there were still good people out there who were optimistic, positive in their perspectives on life and on people. He and his brothers could use a little more of that positivity and innocence in their lives.

That thought suddenly brought feelings of protectiveness and concern over Brighid. She was their woman now, and she would come first in all they did. He never wanted her to lose that love of life, that thinking that more good people and good things occurred in life than bad, and he hoped she never experienced anything evil or that caused her pain.

He brought her hands to his lips and kissed them as the doctor finished up. She smiled at him, and nothing had ever felt more perfect in his life.

* * * *

Brighid stood by with her arms crossed as Pat insisted he didn't need help putting on a pair of scrubs the doctor had given him to go home in. As he teetered and scrunched his face, indicating he was indeed in pain, she exhaled in annoyance.

Rusty leaned next to him. "Take my shoulder tough guy."

Pat growled, but he did take his shoulder to lean on as he stepped into the pants.

"You're so stubborn. Why won't you let me help you?" she asked him.

"Don't, Brighid. Just let me do this."

She uncrossed her arms and was about to continue to argue with him, but then one strong arm came around her waist, and she gasped. Pat and Rusty didn't even look up. They had obviously seen Reece coming.

She pressed back against him, and his arm tightened as he kissed her neck.

"I thought that was my girl's sexy ass in this tight dress. I think we're going to have to talk about your choice in business attire." He suckled the skin on her neck, making her shiver.

"Reece." She exhaled. "Are you okay?" she asked, voice cracking.

He loosened his hold, and she turned in his arms and saw his arm was in a sling. She carefully touched it and covered her mouth with her other hand.

"Oh God."

He placed his hand on her hip. "Shh, baby, I'm fine. It's just a bad sprain, no fracture or anything."

"Well, what did the doctor say? What do you need to do? Can I help in any way?"

He cupped her cheek and gave a soft smile. "There's nothing to do but just let it heal, take some over-the-counter pain relief, and rest it. It's good, Brighid."

She started to feel as if they didn't want her near them. Like maybe she shouldn't have come here to the hospital. Their relationship was brand spanking new. Had she overstepped the boundaries here in the dating-four-men kind of relationship? She felt hurt, confused.

"Fuck, I got it, Rusty. Let's get this shit over with," Pat said, and they started to head out of the room to the main area, where their friends were waiting to see them and show support. As was the media.

She felt out of place as she walked with them and the crowd of people bombarded them.

She stepped aside and watched, wondering why they seemed to be putting distance between them and her.

It took quite some time for the interviews and for their bosses to discuss things with them. She figured it was best for her to leave before they were whisked off to give their statements to police and to the investigators. As she waited for an opportunity to tell them she was heading out, an arm came around her waist, scaring her. She gasped and grabbed onto the arm.

"Hey, it's only me," Tobin said and turned her around and held her shoulders.

She tried swallowing hard and blinking the tears from her eyes, but one look at Tobin's serious expression and she knew he'd seen them.

"Hey, they're fine. My brothers are tough as nails."

She nodded. She was feeling more and more like some weak female who over exaggerated her concern for her four lovers. Maybe that was it. They were only lovers, nothing more right now because they'd made love for two days and hadn't even gone out on a date. That had to be it. None of them had expected her to be here and to be so concerned. They might even think she was playing it up.

"I'm glad you're here. I need to get back to work. I can't even get close enough to the guys to let them know."

"You don't need to leave. I'm sure their chiefs and Pat's commander will tell them to come to their jobs tomorrow to file paperwork etcetera."

She shook her head and lowered her eyes. "I think I should go. I'm really just in the way, and like I said, I have stuff to do at work."

He looked disappointed and then looked behind her at the crowd of reporters and people.

"You're probably right. It's a madhouse. I can drop you off."

"No. That's okay. I'll grab a bus on the corner. No worries."

He pressed his lips to hers. "Thanks for coming and being here for them. I'll see you tonight."

"We'll see," she said, and saw his facial expression and that hardness, that unreadable, deep expression that made her think he didn't trust her or believe her. She hurried out of there and down the street, hoping to keep the tears at bay. But as she reached the corner and threw on her sunglasses, the tears rolled down her cheeks. She felt incomplete. As though she'd done something wrong or she'd thought of their relationship differently than they did. They'd seemed so happy to see her at first, and then they'd pushed her away and distanced themselves. Maybe this wouldn't work out after all.

* * * *

"What do you mean she's not coming over?" Reece asked Rusty.

"I don't know, something about being behind at work because she left today to go to the hospital to see us," Rusty replied.

"She was acting funny when I got to the room," Reece said to them.

"Probably because Pat was being a stubborn dick," Rusty stated.

"I was not."

"You were, too, and wouldn't let her help you," Reece said to him.

"So this is my fault?" Pat asked, throwing his hands up in the air.

"You insulted her."

"So did you, Rusty, and you, too, Reece, by not keeping her by our sides when we were swarmed by the media."

They were all quiet a moment, and then Pat spoke up.

"I hurt her feelings. Holy shit, I was so worried about not looking weak in her eyes that I was pushing her away. I also didn't want those cameras taking pictures of her. You never know what the media might do or say when they see ménage couples in the spotlight. We don't know if she has any family or if having our relationship televised would be negative for her."

"We have to make her understand that we were protecting her and protecting ourselves. This is new to us, too. We've never had a serious relationship and shared a woman like Brighid. It's understandable to hold back and to get cold feet," Reece said.

"God knows what's going through her head right now. We should call her," Rusty added.

"We should call Tobin and tell him to stop by her office and bring her back here," Rusty stated.

"He's caught up with the investigation into the fire. You heard what Jake said about it being suspicious," Pat said to them.

"Well, that was pretty fucking obvious by the two separate explosions," Reece said. "I know the first might have been due to an old boiler system, but damn, the second was something separate and not normal in a fire like that. It's amazing that the adjacent buildings didn't go up in flames, too."

"It was a four-alarm fire," Rusty said. "The second the call came over the radio that an office was down and an explosion had rocked the main streets, everyone got there to assist. It's amazing that more people weren't killed."

"Well, if it is arson, I hope they find the fuckers responsible," Pat said, and they all agreed.

Chapter 6

Arson Investigator Jon Sanders tapped his finger on the printout. He was at the fire training facility and main office with two other investigators. "Look at this. It came over the Internet this morning through our fire call system. A fire in Treasure Town, New Jersey, and the same insurance company that is connected to the two fires here in Connecticut," Jon said to Jeffrey Stone and Gregory Voight.

"Holy crap, that's another link we need," Gregory said.

"Well, we've got ourselves a name that connects the four female fire victims and him, thanks to that trip out to New Hampshire. All four of those women were seeing a man with the same description as the boyfriend of our last victim, Gracie May. It has to be our arsonist," Jeffrey said to them.

"Okay, so what do we do from here? We can't get a location of residence, only a name," Gregory said.

"We have a picture of the guy and his name. Let's run it through the system and see what we get," John Sanders said to them as he started typing on the computer.

"I think if we put in these details and last known address as Hartford, Connecticut, and we can take it from there. With this new system, if he ever started a fire, called up about a fire, was hospitalized or processed for a crime, it will come up. Hell, if he got a ticket for no seatbelt or was late returning a library book, it could come up on here."

"And to think with a system like that there are still assholes getting away with murder and arson," Gregory said.

"You're not kidding," Jeffrey said.

"Bingo, looks like we have two pages of shit," John said and scrolled down, looking for more info to nab this guy.

"Here we go. Let's see what we have here. Okay, looks like he's been in and out of trouble since about thirteen years old. Petty larceny, oh, yeah, look at this. He started a fire in the boys' bathroom at the high school he attended."

"Click onto that file." Jeffrey pointed. "It shows more information."

"Yeah, but it's with the juvenile courts system. It won't give much more than what can be disclosed at public records. Write this number down and this case number. If we call up, they could give us more info to help with the investigation," Gregory told Jeffrey, who wrote it down.

"Scroll farther. Anything else on there?" Gregory asked.

John scrolled further. "Just some illegal parking tickets."

"Wait, can you see where those were? Does it give an exact location?"

John looked and clicked onto the next screen.

"Gives addresses in town and the exact spot. Why?"

"Look at that address. That's right down the block from the fire that started in the storefront," Gregory said.

"Coincidence?" John asked.

"What's the likelihood of that?" Jeffrey said. "Scroll farther and see the others. Gregory, call that number and find out what's in that closed case file. If anything, this can all lead up to strengthening the profile of this guy Stark and show motive to committing these crimes. Right now, at minimum, we can bring him in for questioning in regards to the deaths of four women he was with."

"Why wouldn't the investigators in the case look at him as a prime suspect? He was the shared factor in all cases," John said.

"Maybe simply because no one knew this guy Stark was the boyfriend of those other women at the time. Remember, we only found out that the last two victims had a boyfriend who was hardly ever seen. He probably made them keep their relationship a secret."

"Which could also explain why the victims were burned first and appeared to be tied to a bed when their homes were set on fire. It could be some sexual fantasy for the killer since those fires started on the beds.," John said to them.

"But the fires on the businesses have no connections to these women or to Stark. The only connection between them is that the same chemical substance residue was found at all crime scenes, including the ones where the women were killed.," John added.

"I don't get it yet either, but making a call to the investigators involved with the fire in Treasure Town yesterday is definitely a necessity, especially because of the shared insurance name between the business fires," Gregory said.

"Let's call right now. We have the names of three investigators involved. There's a Trent Landers, arson investigator, a Detective Buddy Landers, and a Detective Tobin McQuinn. Let's see what they have so far and maybe we need to head out there while the fire is still fresh," John said and then made the call.

* * * *

Tobin sat in the conference room with Trent and Buddy Landers. Some state police investigators and an arson investigator were interested in details about the fire at the local gift shop. As they explained their cases and the similarities, Leisure Insurance Company came up again. That was where Brighid worked, and immediately his gut clenched with concern. Last night she'd said she couldn't come over because she had a lot of paperwork to do and mistakes to correct. His investigative mind was starting to worry. When the investigators suggested they come out to have a look around, and hopefully be there when the forensic results came in, he was even more concerned.

"Are you thinking somehow that this insurance company could be part of insurance fraud and this guy, this arsonist, is also connected?" Buddy Landers asked Investigator Gregory Voight.

"We've been at this for months. Although it seems like two separate incidences, there are links between the two sets of suspicious fires and homicides," Voight told them.

"What's this guy's connection to Leisure Insurance?" Trent asked and glanced at Tobin. He could tell his friends were concerned to say the least and probably wondering about Brighid and who she worked for.

"Not sure if there is one. We do know that the victims were in a relationship, though hidden, with this individual. Have you gotten any preliminary results of the samples you took from the fire at the gift shop in your town?" Gregory asked.

"We should have them by tomorrow latest. We did notice some discoloration near the boiler system. There appeared to be some fuel leaking but nothing that could start that fire and cause such an explosion. We gathered samples of the silt around it and some white residue with ash."

The investigator was silent a moment.

"We're going to be heading down today. Should get there by tonight. Could we meet at the department in the morning first thing?" John Sanders asked.

"We'll be here," Trent said, and then they disconnected the call.

Tobin took a deep breath and exhaled.

"Okay, sounds like they have more info and aren't ready to put it out to us," Trent said to them.

"I agree, but I don't like the fact that Leisure Insurance could be connected. They just moved their business into town, and a lot of people are going to them from this community," Tobin said.

Buddy leaned back in his chair and looked at Tobin.

"You and your brothers just started seeing a woman that works there," Buddy said.

Tobin held his gaze and didn't respond verbally.

"Let's look at this in as many ways as we can so we're on the same page here. That business has had customers from our town for years. They were based in Connecticut, where these other fires occurred and payoffs were made. This guy, whoever he is, doesn't seem to have a connection to the insurance company. The investigators said this guy was involved with every woman who was killed.. Had his car illegally parked a day before down the block from that fire's location. If the two cases are connected, we need to find the common factor," Trent said to them.

"What if we get the name of the guy and a picture of him and ask the owners, the workers at the insurance company if he's a client, if they know him, et cetera?" Tobin asked.

"We could do that, or we sit tight until tomorrow morning since it's after hours, and let these investigators share what they have, and we try to solve this and prove there's no connection. I'd hate to think that Bricker Daily worked with an insurance company to get money. People could have been killed. Your brothers could have been," Buddy replied.

"I know, and it was pretty damn scary. Two other stores could have gone up in flames. Maybe I can ask Brighid some questions about that company she works for?" Tobin asked.

"Not sure if that's such a smart idea," Buddy said.

"Why not?" Tobin asked.

"You don't really know her, Tobin. None of us do, and the fact that she works for a company that could have a connection to two arson investigations in Connecticut, and now this one here in Treasure Town, isn't something to take lightly."

"There's no way Brighid is involved with this. I'm telling you I know people, and she's a good person. Sweet, kind of sees the world in a positive light. It's one of the things my brothers and I like best about her." He shook his head.

"My gut is never off. She's not part of this, and asking her some questions could get us answers we need," Tobin replied.

"What if those questions lead you to thinking she is involved? Will you be able to handle it professionally?" Trent asked.

Tobin thought about that for a moment, along with the fact that his brothers could have lost their lives the other day.

"If she is involved, I'm the last person she'd want in a room alone with her. My brothers could have died."

* * * *

Brighid ignored their phone calls and text messages, and now she was headed to work, hoping to get through the day. She couldn't believe that the fire had been at the gift shop that it belonged to Bricker Daily. She had a terrible feeling in the pit of her stomach, and she couldn't shake the feeling that her bosses were up to no good and doing illegal shit. She thought about telling Tobin, but if her bosses were involved with insurance fraud, she wouldn't want her boyfriend dragged into it and used by some judge as a reason to dismiss the case. She needed someone who didn't know her or have a connection to her.

When she thought about going to the local authorities, she felt sick. What if her bosses were legit? What if the circumstances were misconstrued by her imagination and love of mystery? Then, of course, she worried about her job and having no security. What would she do? Where would she work and get money? Where would she live? She hadn't known the men long enough to crash into their lives, especially after the way they'd treated her and acted at the hospital. They wanted space. They wouldn't ask her to live with them.

Her heart felt heavy as walked out of her condo and over to her car. The last person she expected to see was Tobin.

She unlocked her car door, opened the back door, and placed her bags inside. She closed the door.

He stood there with his arms crossed, his badge, gun giving an instant air of authority and power. She swallowed hard as she absorbed his attire, dress pants, dress shirt, sporting his sexy good looks and sensational body. Her pussy throbbed. She missed him and his brothers.

"We've been worried," he said in that deep, hard tone that was all Tobin.

"Why?"

He raised one of his eyebrows up at her. "It's been three days. We've called, and we've texted. No response. What's wrong?"

She didn't know why, but the tears filled her eyes. Her idea of being strong and ignoring the pull in her heart and in her professional life was taking its toll.

"If you're in some kind of trouble and you need help, I'm here for you."

Why would he say such a thing to her?

"What?"

He uncrossed his arms and reached out to take her hand.

"You look about ready to burst into tears. It has to be bad, so tell me, and I'll help you."

She shook her head. "It's hard to just say it."

"Just do it," he pushed.

"I don't want to come across clingy or needy because I get that you guys don't want me to be so deep into your lives and that you want space. It's just hard for me to not want to be with you and to care about you, and it hurts to know that you can so easily push me away and keep your distance. I was only trying to show how much I care and not be sappy. But I've never been involved in a serious relationship, never mind with four men at once, and to tell you the truth, the four of you intimidate me. I don't think I can handle a relationship like that."

"Whoa, slow down, baby. Jesus, what in God's name are you rambling on about? Clingy? Not wanting you close, deep in our lives?

That's not true at all. Damn, my brothers weren't kidding when they said they fucked things up with you."

"What do you mean?"

"I mean they said they were trying not to make you feel uncomfortable with the reporters and the crowds of people at the hospital that day. They didn't know if you wanted the relationship between us to be public, that maybe you had family and they might not be too keen on a ménage relationship. Plus, Pat was feeling vulnerable, and he doesn't do vulnerable well, none of us do, and he didn't want you to see him weak." He cupped her cheeks and pressed her against her car. She held on to his waist as the tears rolled down her cheeks.

"Damn, they were being buffoons. We want you in our lives. We're so pissed you haven't called or texted back. We want you in our lives as much as possible. Hell, we want you in our beds and in our house with us, but we know it's too soon to ask that kind of commitment from you."

"Really?" she asked, lip quivering.

He smiled softly and then covered her mouth and kissed her deeply. That went on for minutes until they finally had to stop and breathe and remember they were in a parking lot.

He pressed his forehead to hers while he kept his arms around her waist.

"Is there anything else going on that has you concerned and not wanting to return our calls and text messages?" he asked, and she felt her heart racing. He pulled back.

"Brighid?"

She swallowed hard.

He clutched her chin and held her gaze with a firm expression.

"It's fine, Tobin. I'm just being silly, and I tend to see a mystery in things when there isn't. Look what I did with you guys, thinking that you don't want me so deeply involved with your lives."

"It sounds like more than that, and it's not silly if it's something that's worrying you."

"I don't want to get you involved if it is something."

"Hey, if there is reason for you to be worried or concerned, I want you to know that my brothers and I are here for you. We can help and work it out. What is it?"

"I don't want to make accusations that could get people into trouble. I'd hate to think that certain things are going on and shouldn't be."

"Are you talking about work?"

"Yes."

"Okay, are you having a hard time telling me because I'm your boyfriend or because I'm a detective?" he asked.

"Boyfriend," she told him.

He released her and stepped back and crossed his arms in front of his chest.

"Okay, Miss Murphy, what seems to have you feeling concerned over work?" he asked, and she tilted her head sideways at him and crossed her arms in front of her chest.

"Really, Tobin?"

"That's Detective McQuinn, ma'am. What are your concerns?"

She stared at him and debated about telling him everything she feared and suspected.

"I don't want you involved, Tobin. If there is something bad, illegal, going on then a judge could find out that you and I are involved and get charges dropped if charges are necessary."

"Okay, listen, it sounds serious, and I get your worry for me, but this is my job. I have friends, other detectives that work with me. If you tell them what's going on, and I agree that me being lead in this could be a negative, then we change things around and I introduce you to the right people. How does that sound?"

"You can do that?"

"Of course. Now explain."

* * * *

With every detail of Brighid's suspicions, he felt his gut clench and his heart pound. She didn't know it yet, but she'd just provided a bunch of information that, if documented and copied, could prove that insurance fraud was indeed involved with the local fire and the others out of town in Connecticut. But how could he keep her from being pulled in as a co-conspirator in this, especially as she mentioned her password being used and items being changed.

"I took some screen shots of everything and even the times that someone logged into my computer. Then I changed the password."

"Have your bosses asked you what the new password is yet?"

"No."

He ran his hand along his mouth.

"Okay, I don't want you to do anything but your job there. Don't ask questions. Don't look for more evidence. Just leave that to us and the investigators. I'm going to talk to my people and see about setting up a meeting with you and them. But I would like for the investigators to run this like you're a suspect. That way your bosses won't be onto what's really going on here."

"Will that work? I mean the last couple of days they've been out and about like they don't have a worry in the world. I could be wrong and imagining all this stuff."

"You had a gut feeling that something wasn't right when Bricker Daily showed up with a check at the office. You knew he was never a client yet connected the night someone logged into your computer and altered payments and added Bricker as a client for the past three years. You're not imagining things. You're giving the detectives the proof they need to ask for warrants, to come in and confiscate documents and computers to prove insurance fraud."

"Oh God, Tobin. I don't know if I can handle this." She covered her mouth with her hand.

He pulled her close and gave her shoulders a squeeze as he held her gaze, her green eyes misty with tears. "You can do this because those men, and this arsonist, whoever he is, could have killed three of your boyfriends. We could have lost Pat, Rusty, and Reece. If that isn't motivation to put these men responsible behind bars, baby, then I don't know what is."

She looked so serious, and he watched the tears fall from her eyes.

"I love them, and I love you. I'll do it. I'll help however I can."

He pulled her close and hugged her and prayed that he and the investigators could gather the evidence necessary to put the men responsible behind bars.

* * * *

It was hard for Brighid to play dumb the entire day at work, but she did it, despite having to file the documents and sign off on the material to put the insurance claim forward to the investigative department on the Bricker Daily case. She also needed to call the police department and talk with the investigators involved. A Detective Buddy Landers told her that they were still working on the investigation and that arson investigator, Trent Landers, was waiting on results from forensic samples left at the scene. She wrote notes and added them to the file and then placed it into the cabinet. As she closed up the cabinet and turned around, Lenny was there.

"How are we doing on closing the Daily file?" he asked. She was surprised at how he'd snuck up on her.

She gave him an odd expression. "Lenny, these things take time, sometimes weeks or months, depending on the circumstances. It's nowhere near closed."

"Did you issue the temporary money to Mr. Daily while he waits for the process to complete?"

"It's been a little more than forty-eight hours. Money will not be released that quickly in a case like this one."

"Shit." He ran his fingers through his hair.

"What's wrong, Lenny? You know how this works. Why would this case be any different?"

"I was just hoping to get him and his family some money sooner than later. Maybe I'll just loan him some for now to pay his bills and things."

"That's very nice of you, but why would he need help? He ran a good business. The investigations showed he was up to date on mortgage payments and wasn't behind in anything. The initial reports show decent income."

"Well, not everything is accurate on paper. Don't worry. I'll take care of it. I know there's no way to speed things up," Lenny said.

"I wish there was, but this is how the system works. Did you have anything else for me to handle tonight? I have plans."

"With one of the firefighters or the cop?" he asked, and her heart pounded.

"Would you believe all three of them and a fourth older brother?" she asked and then began to walk past him.

"Seriously, Brighid?" he asked and looked her body over in a different way than ever before. It made her gain such an attitude. How dare he judge her or question her love life?

"Well, you told me to go out and get a social life. So I did."

"Four men, together, with you?" he asked. His eyes roamed over her breasts, and then he licked his lips and smirked.

"Four very possessive, protective men, who don't take a liking to any other men looking at me, never mind touching me. So, yes, four. I'll see you tomorrow. Get a good night's sleep. I have a feeling this week is going to be a long one."

She left him there looking like an idiot. She, on the other hand, couldn't wait to get the hell out of there and go home and change. As she went outside, she was surprised to see Tobin's truck parked right next to hers.

His window was rolled down, and he gave her body the once-over before he spoke. "I'll follow you home and then drive you to our place. The guys can't wait to see you."

She gave a wave and added a little extra wiggle to her walk, knowing that Tobin was staring at her ass. She hadn't expected him to honk the horn, which was deep and loud, so she jumped and then gave him a sassy look.

"Don't worry, darling. I'll be smacking that sexy ass in just a little while. We sure do need to talk about your wardrobe for work."

She waved her hand at him, as if indication of "whatever" then got into her car and chuckled. He revved the truck's diesel engine, and she revved her convertible's engine and off they went.

Once they got to her condo and were inside, Tobin locked the door and started explaining about where they were in the case and what the investigators thought about her information. They were meeting tomorrow morning to go over the findings of the lab results that should have been in yesterday.

She went into the walk-in closet and started to unzip her dress.

She told him about what Lenny had asked today and also about his reaction to her telling him she was involved with all four men. She eased back and tried to unzip the dress until she felt Tobin's hands there helping her. She looked at him through the reflection in the mirror.

"He looked at you like he was undressing you with his eyes?" He pulled the zipper all the way down, and she let her arms hang as the material pooled to the rug below.

"What would you expect him to do? He's a man."

Tobin ran his hands up her back to her bra and unclipped it. She stared at him through the mirror and watched it fall. Tobin licked his lips and then leaned forward and kissed her shoulder.

"He can't look at, never mind touch, what belongs to me and my brothers."

She tilted her head back, and he ran his hands under her arms to her breasts, cupping them. She moaned from the feel of his big, warm hands.

"Goddamn, baby, I missed these breasts and this body. You belong to me, to the McQuinn brothers."

She pushed her ass back against his crotch as he slowly rocked his hips into her from behind.

"Fuck, we're going to be late. Grab a hold of that dresser in front of you, baby. I need in."

She heard his zipper go down, and he released her from around the waist and then used his thigh to spread her wider. She did immediately and gripped the dresser in front of her and let him pull her hips back. His fingers found her pussy and clit. They moved back and forth across the sensitive nub and then stroked into her pussy.

She was coming already, and he wasn't even in her. She was so, desperate for him to fill her up with his cock.

"Please, Tobin, I need you now."

"Fuck yeah." He pulled his fingers from her pussy, aligned his cock with it, and then gripped her hips and shoved in deep. He immediately pulled back and shoved in again and again.

"Fuck yeah, I love watching you in that mirror. Look at those tits bob up and down while I fuck this pussy."

Smack, smack, smack.

"Oh God. Oh!" She screamed as she came hard. Tobin didn't slow down his pace. He kept stroking and thrusting into her over and over again. Their bodies slapped against one another, and she felt his cock grow thicker, harder.

"Oh sweet God, yes, yes, baby, you feel so tight, so fucking good. Fuck." He yelled out and stroked into her three more times, so hard she nearly lost her grip on the dresser when he filled her with his seed as he came.

He pressed his head against her back and kissed her skin while massaging her ass.

"I love you, baby. Know that, always."

He eased out, and she turned around and hugged him tightly around his midsection. "I love you too, Tobin. I can't wait to see your brothers."

He gave her ass a slap, she gasped, and then kissed her lips and spoke his words against them. "And they can't wait to see you and make love to you, too."

She smiled wide, and then they jumped into her shower together for another round of lovemaking before they headed to the McQuinn compound.

* * * *

"What's taking them so long to get here?" Pat asked as he sat down by the island in the kitchen, holding a can of beer.

"Is it just me or are you guys worried about her working at the company and being part of the investigation?" Reece asked.

"I'm worried. God knows how deep those dicks she works for are into this shit. I'll be happy when it's over and we can just move on with our lives with her. I want those assholes behind bars," Rusty added.

"We can't make her feel bad for still working there or make her nervous. Tobin assured us that she's safe and that the investigation is really about her bosses and a connection to insurance fraud," Reece said.

"I don't really care, just as long as she's safe and with us. I hope those investigators don't try to pin any shit on her," Pat said.

"Why would they do that when she's helping them? She gave information about the files being altered, and thank God she was smart enough to take those screen shots," Rusty said.

"You're not kidding, or this could be a worse situation and they could look at her as part of this illegal operation," Reece stated.

They all looked toward the door as they heard the truck pull up out front.

"Damn, it's like having a first fucking date, but we've already fucked her, so why am I so damn nervous?" Pat rubbed his sweaty palms on his thighs.

"Because the last time you saw her, you pushed her away and made her feel like we didn't want people to know she was our woman," Reece told him, and Rusty chuckled as Pat growled low. Reece smirked. But then the door opened, and Tobin and Brighid entered.

"Damn, baby, I missed you." Reece pulled her close and kissed her deeply.

Pat watched, feeling his cock instantly harden at the sight of her. She was fucking perfection from her sexy eyes to that luscious, curvy body.

She pulled back. "Where is your sling?"

"I don't need it."

Rusty stepped forward and pulled her into his arms. "He needs it, but he won't use it." He rolled his eyes at Reece and then smiled at Brighid as he cupped her cheek and held her at her waist.

"You look beautiful, as always." He leaned down and kissed her lips, and she hugged him tightly after he kissed her.

Pat stood up, feeling only a little ache to the back of his thighs from the stitches. Rusty let her go, and she remained where she was.

"How are you feeling, Pat? Still in some pain?" she asked.

"I'm good, doll. The only pain I feel is missing having you in my arms and in my bed. Get your ass over here," he stated firmly, and she moved so quickly, hugging him tightly and burrowing into his neck, that he nearly lost his balance. He ran his hands along her back and her ass and lifted her up into his arms. She pulled back, and then their gazes locked and she kissed him. She held his cheeks in her hands and continued to kiss him. He turned her toward the wall in the kitchen and knocked down a picture frame as she straddled his waist and he rocked against her hips. Their lips parted, and they were practically gasping for air.

"Oh God, baby, I need you. We all need to be inside of you."

"Yes. I need you all, too. I missed you. You got me so mad, made me think that you didn't want me fully."

"Never, baby. We want you in this house, in our bed, and in every aspect of our lives," he told her, and she kissed him again as she rocked her hips up and down against him.

"Can you carry her to the bedroom, or do you need help?" Rusty asked.

"Fuck you, I don't need help. She's as light as a feather."

She ran her fingers through his hair and held his gaze. "Your stitches. Are you going to be able to make love to me?" she asked, filled with concern. He could see it in her face and in her bright green eyes.

"Baby, no fucking stitches are going to keep me from fucking this pussy and this ass tonight. So get yourself ready. You're in for a very long night of lovemaking."

He carried her up the stairs and felt the pinching sensation from the stitches, but he would be damned if it stopped him from fucking his woman until she cried out his name as she came.

He set her feet down and worked at taking her clothes off. She undid his pants and then pulled his shirt up over his head. Rusty unzipped her pants and helped her step out of them and her panties. Reece unbuttoned her blouse and leaned down to suckle her breast as Rusty unclipped her bra. She was naked and moaning as Pat started to try and step out of his pants. He was kicking them off as he grabbed her waist, turned her around, and bent her forward. Rusty was holding his cock, stroking it as he sat on the edge of the bed.

"Suck Rusty's cock, baby," Pat told her, and she ran her hands along Rusty's thighs and licked his cock. Pat watched Rusty grab a hold of her hair and her head then thrust upward.

Pat finally got his pants all the way off, and he fell to his knees behind her and ran his hands up her smooth thighs and between her legs, spreading her. He sought out her pussy and stroked a finger deep, in and out, as she moaned and pushed her ass back at him. Tobin came over and ran his palm along her ass.

"She's got a good spanking coming her way. She should have spoken to us about how we made her feel instead of sulking and ignoring our texts and calls. She also got herself in the middle of a little situation at work, and any danger is not acceptable as far as she's concerned. You ready to accept your punishment, Brighid?" Tobin asked, squeezing her ass cheeks apart.

She moaned and nodded as she continued to suck Rusty's cock.

Smack, smack, smack.

The sound of Tobin's palm landing on her ass cheek echoed in the room. She jerked back as Pat continued to finger her pussy from behind. A gush of cream leaked from her cunt, and Pat felt his cock grow harder.

Smack, smack, smack. Tobin gave another set of smacks to her ass, turning the other cheek a nice shade of pink.

"Goddamn, that is sexy as hell," Reece chimed in and ran his palm along her ass cheeks and right to her anus. He pulled out a tube of lube and squirted some onto his finger.

"Get ready, baby. Three at a time is coming your way."

"Oh fuck, baby, slow down," Rusty complained.

Pat pulled his fingers from her cunt as Reece pressed a lubricated digit to her anus.

Smack, smack, smack.

"Oh God!" She moaned after pulling from Rusty's cock.

"Now. I need her fucking now," Pat demanded.

Rusty lifted her up by her waist, and she sank down onto his cock in one stroke. She gripped his shoulders and began to rock on top of him as Pat grabbed lube from Reece. He added some to her ass and his fingers and stroked them into her ass from behind.

"Yes! Yes, Pat, more," she said, egging him on.

"Come here, baby. I've got something for you," Reece told her as he pulled her down so she could suck his cock. She licked the tip and then began to suck him down.

Pat couldn't hold back. The sights and the sounds were so arousing that even Tobin was stroking his cock and running his hands along her back as their brothers fucked her.

Pat pulled his fingers from her ass and replaced them with his cock. He could hardly breathe as he slowly began to push into her ass. She pushed back, and that was the end for him. Pat began to thrust and rock into her ass in sync with Rusty's and Reece's thrusts.

"Fuck, I'm there. Holy fucking shit." Reece held his cock into her mouth and came.

Pat felt his cock enlarge, and then Brighid cried out her release as Pat thrust hard and came.

Rusty held her close and rocked up and down until Pat pulled out and Tobin took his place. Pat sat on the bed and watched as Tobin gripped her hips and rubbed his cock back and forth against her anus.

"Please, oh God, Tobin, I need you."

"You need what?" he asked and spanked her ass twice on each cheek.

"You inside of me."

"But Rusty is inside of you, baby," he teased her, and she rocked her hips back as Tobin continued to rub his cock over her well-lubricated anus.

"Tobin, damn it, I need your cock in my ass now. Do it!" she demanded, and Pat and Reece chuckled as Rusty pinched her nipples, making her gasp and cry out.

"As you please, baby," Tobin said and then pressed his cock to her anus and slid right in.

Reece got up and walked out of the room. He came back with a washcloth and towel, wiping his cock off. "I need my woman again." He sat on the bed and stroked her hair.

"You see this, baby? You see how hard and needy my cock is?" he asked, and she moaned and nodded. "It's you. You do it to me. I need you so badly. I need to fuck that sweet, wet pussy until you call out my name. You hear me, baby?"

"Yes. Oh God, yes, Reece."

"Fuck," both Tobin and Rusty said as they both came inside of her.

Tobin pulled from her ass, and Rusty rolled her to her back.

Reece pulled her to him and kissed her deeply. He spread her legs wide and slid right into her cunt with no hesitation.

"Oh Reece. Reece," she exclaimed as he widened her thighs and began to thrust into her pussy faster and deeper, making the bed creak and moan.

"You're all ours, Brighid. You're our woman now, you got that?"

"Yes, yes, Reece. Oh God, you're so hard."

"You make me hard," he said through clenched teeth and then suckled against her neck. She cried out another release, and Reece followed as he grunted and thrust until he couldn't move. He lay over her on his elbows, trying not to crush her.

"I love you so much, baby. You were made for us."

She smiled softly and then wrapped her arms around his neck and hugged him to her breasts.

"I love you too, Reece. I love all of you."

* * * *

Bridget got out of the shower, and Reece was there, holding a towel for her. He pulled her into his arms and hugged her tightly.

"I missed not having you around for a few days. It was torture."

She smiled and felt the butterflies in her belly. She had truly missed them, too. They'd missed valuable time they could have been making love and talking, getting to know one another.

"I missed you, too. I guess I learned that when something is bothering me that I need to talk to you guys."

"That's true, baby, and we need to talk to you if something is bothering us." He helped her to dry off.

"Oh, my clothes are in the bedroom."

"No need. I've got something right here." Reece gave her a T-shirt.

"Engine 18, huh?" She ran her hand along his arm and saw the bruising there. "Are you sure you don't need to be wearing that sling?"

He cupped her breasts and leaned forward, licking the tip of one. "Did it stop me from being able to make love to you?"

She shook her head. "Then enough said. Put this on. The others are downstairs waiting for us for dinner."

She lifted the shirt up over her head, and Reece ran a finger along her pussy and belly, making her giggle being caught off guard. She got the T-shirt on and scolded him.

"Reece!" she exclaimed and ran after him. When she got through the door to the bedroom, he had moved to the side, and as she realized, he bent down and tipped her over his shoulder.

"Reece, put me down."

"No way, baby. Don't you know what this hold is called?" He ran his hand along her ass as he walked down the stairs as if she were light as a feather.

"The fireman's hold. Works real well," he said as he entered the kitchen. His finger pressed against her pussy, and she reached back and slapped his hand.

"I don't think the fireman's hold involves your finger going there."

He quickly brought her back down to her feet, making her head spin as she gasped and held on to his forearms. He pulled her close and kissed her as he ran his hands along her ass, squeezing them under the T-shirt.

"When I use it on you, it sure as shit does."

She gave his forearm a slap and turned around, only for Rusty to pull her onto his lap. He looked at her shirt and then shook his head at his brother. "Really? Engine 18?"

"Jealous?" Reece asked as he popped a piece of potato into his mouth before he sat down to join them.

"Why would I be when Engine 20 is better?" he shot at Reece. "Don't worry, baby. I'll get you one of my shirts to wear from my company."

"Don't be silly. If it gets you upset, I'll borrow one of Tobin's or Pat's shirts."

"Yeah, a Treasure Town PD shirt. There's two of us anyway, so she can wear it," Pat said to them.

"That's ridiculous. How will people know she's ours?" Rusty said as he ran his hand up and down her thigh.

"People already know she's ours, and those who don't will know soon enough," Tobin said very seriously, but he gave her a wink. She smiled.

"I like it that she's wearing my shirt. So leave it on," Recce said.

"She'll take turns wearing our shirts. How about that?" Rusty teased as if he were making fun of Reece.

"Why not just get a shirt with all our logos on it? Everyone will know she belongs to two firefighters and two cops. She can be a fucking billboard for first responders," Pat snapped at them.

"I can beat that," Brighid stated, and they all looked at her. She stood up and ran her hands along her shirt and pulled it out as if she were reading it.

"It can say, Property of the McQuinn Brothers."

She plopped down into the empty seat between Reece and Rusty and took a sip from her glass.

"I love it. How fast can we get it made up?" Pat asked.

"We'll need it in every color because it's the only thing she'll wear with bottoms like jeans or a skirt," Tobin said.

"I know a guy who can get it done by tomorrow in at least four colors," Rusty said to them.

"I say we just get it tattooed on her lower back. Then everyone will know when she's on the beach in her bikini and she's not wearing one of the shirts." Reece ran his hand along her thigh under the table.

"I was only kidding. Get real. I am not wearing a shirt that says I am the property of anyone," she scolded, and they held her gaze, looked super serious, and then they started laughing.

"I say we just make sure she has one of us with her at all times. That ought to do it," Reece said, and they all agreed.

They started to eat dinner, passing out steaks Tobin had cooked on the grill as she showered. They talked about their jobs and what their commanders wanted them to do in order to return to active duty.

"I have to make sure I can physically lift shit and do a bunch of stupid crap. But I'll be fine to start in two days," Reece told her.

"I have to wait until these stitches get taken out and the doctors, both in the hospital and the police department physician, give the okay. I think by Friday. Not sure," Pat said.

"I just need for the stitches to be removed. Maybe a few more days but I can do the job. They'll probably play it safe and make me wait longer."

"That was so crazy how that fire and the explosions happened. We could hear them from the office, and when I heard the sirens, I was so worried about you guys, and I didn't even know if you would be the ones responding," she said to them.

"It wasn't a normal fire, that's for shit sure," Rusty said as he played with the rim of his glass.

"No it wasn't. I haven't seen or been in a fire like that in several years, like when that blaze was set on purpose over at the abandoned warehouse by the swamp," Reece added.

Brighid felt instantly sick to her stomach. She had been so worried when she knew they were injured, but then to find out that her boss could be somehow involved with the fire was eating her up inside.

She placed her fork down and then looked up to see them all watching her. Rusty reached out and caressed her hair.

"We're not going to lie. We're worried about you going to that job of yours. It isn't safe. Those men you work for could have something to do with this," he said to her.

"I don't really want to work there anymore, knowing what could have possibly gone down, but if it helps to secure a criminal case, then I really should stay there," she said.

"But you don't have to. Let the investigators handle it. They need to gather the evidence and prove arson and insurance fraud. We want you safe." Reece took her hand and brought it to her lips.

"I know you do, but if I leave now, for no reason at all, then they'll get suspicious, and it could screw things up. Tobin said that the investigators got here tonight from Connecticut and should be making plans to go by the firm tomorrow and start issuing subpoenas and begin gathering evidence. They're following their protocol. It's better that I'm there and it looks like I didn't know anything about them coming or that I shared my suspicions with Tobin and the investigators from the state police."

"I don't like it." Rusty stood up from the table. "How can you ensure her safety, Tobin? We don't even know who the arsonist is."

"They have a name," Tobin said, "and they did research on the guy and are making connections to other stuff. They'll find him. In the meantime, this insurance fraud situation is pretty big. If they can get her bosses and charge them, then they could get more information on this arsonist they hired to do these fires. Then the state police and arson investigators from Connecticut can arrest the guy and charge him with numerous other arson fires and charges, including murder."

"Murder?" she asked, shocked that this was the first she was hearing about it.

"Yes, Brighid. The investigators believe that the person who your bosses hired to start these fires to collect insurance money is the same person they're after for a set of five fires where five women were killed. From what I gathered from the investigators from Connecticut, there was a similar substance—a residue—that was found at all the crime scenes linking them."

"Goddamn, they think this is the same guy?" Reece asked.

"Then he's somewhere in town as we speak," Rusty added.

"What does he look like? Can you get a hold of a picture?" Pat asked Tobin.

"I can tomorrow when I meet with the investigators and our team in the morning. I would say by late afternoon we'll have those subpoenas and the search warrants to get a hold of the computers and files in the office, plus phone taps, too."

"So this could all be over by tomorrow night?" Reece asked Tobin.

"It very well could be," Tobin said.

"Then I need to stick with what I'm doing and go to work. It will all be over by tomorrow." She gave Reece and Rusty a reassuring smile.

Rusty sat back down and pulled her close. "Why not call in tomorrow and stay here with us. We could make love all day and snuggle in bed." He kissed along her neck and then her shoulder.

"I can't. I need to be there by eight. I've been getting there early every day, and if I show up late, they'll ask me questions."

"Well then, I say let's clean up from dinner and head straight to bed for dessert," Reece told her, and she chuckled.

She ran her finger along his chin and then she slid off her chair and straddled him. He wrapped his arm around her waist, lifting her shirt in the process.

"I've been doing a lot of thinking lately about where I want to make love to you." He kissed her throat and then her lips.

"Oh really? Like where?" she asked, practically moaning in his embrace.

"What better place to eat you out than on the dinner table?"

She gasped as he lifted her up, placed her onto the table, and lay her down. He spread her thighs and scooted closer right before he licked her bare cunt. She was even more shocked to realize that the others had moved the dishes off the table and made room for him to lay her down. They hadn't said a word. It was as though they could read one another's minds and knew exactly what they wanted. Her, to feast on.

Tobin and Pat leaned over, pushed her shirt upward toward her breasts, and then began to suckle them.

"Now this is a meal I certainly could get used to seeing on the table when I get home from work," Reece said as she moaned from their simultaneous stimulating touches until she couldn't hold back any longer and came.

"Damn, I think I could get very used to this too," she said, and they all chuckled, making her pussy spasm and her heart leap for joy at the love she had for her four very attentive and creative first responders.

Chapter 7

Stark had everything in place. The bed was moved to the center of the basement. The locks, the chains, and bindings for her legs and wrists were secure, and there would be no way she could escape. The house he'd rented for six months was under Lenny's name, the sap. He didn't even know it. Just signed whatever Stark asked him, too. In fact, he'd even paid for most of what Stark had lined up in the house. He gathered all his tools, the table, and the training devices. He wasn't going to give up on Brighid like he did the others. No, Brighid was different. She was stronger, tougher, calmer than the ones before her. She would be his greatest prize, an amazing ending to his career as a paid arsonist.

The other day had been his last job. He'd lost his focus. He screwed up because he was thinking of her, his angel of fire. But it didn't matter anymore. No one would find them. He would take a few days to break her in, to get her to listen and submit to his authority. Then they would leave town, move on to another location and work on their personal bonding time. But first he would show her the power he had and what exactly fire would help him to achieve with her.

He glanced at his watch. It was almost time. She always got to work early, and today would be no different. Today, he would be there waiting for her.

* * * *

Matt Walsh was an auxiliary cop waiting to get hired on as a full-time deputy for the Treasure Town sheriff's department. He was on the list, and basically, doing this job as auxiliary helped him to score points with the big shots and let them know how serious he was about law enforcement. Truth was he didn't have much more time to waste. If they didn't hire him soon, he would have to search for a different profession, preferably one that paid him regularly. So when he got the call from the department this morning about doing some security work for a potential situation that would occur later in the afternoon with some big shots from Connecticut, he figured he better say yes.

It was kind of lame parking here since six a.m. Nothing was happening on the street near the Leisure Insurance Company. There were only a few cars parked and one black van, which had pulled up about fifteen minutes ago and had the word PVT Delivery in white on it. He'd never heard of it, and the van just parked alongside another three spots near the front of the insurance firm. He couldn't really see into the window of the van because they were darkly tinted, but then he noticed two other cars pull up and two men got out, exchanging hellos and never really taking interest in the van, so neither did Mathew.

But then a man opened the door and stepped out of the van. He looked at the cars, and then he looked right at Mathew.

The man had a big smile on his face as he walked across the landscaping and then the road. He came around the side of the police cruiser, and Mathew had his window down.

"Can I help you?" he asked.

"Nope, just waiting on my girl to arrive."

"Your girl?" Mathew asked.

"Yep, and you're going to be a problem."

It was really fast how quickly the man reached up and stuck Mathew in the neck. Mathew felt his body go numb very quickly. The man's face was clear as day, and Mathew would never forget it. He memorized it before he passed out completely.

* * * *

Brighid was listening to the radio and heard about the bad weather coming their way tonight. Lots of heavy rain, winds, thunder, and lightning. The surf was going to be extra rough and the fear for flash flooding high. She would be glad when today was over and she could stay with her men at their place where she would feel safe and warm. She pulled into the parking lot at the office and noticed the police car across the way. Her heart began to race, and she wondered if something was already happening since Lenny and Ray were already there. But there didn't seem to be anyone in the vehicle. She parked between Lenny's car and the black van that she didn't recognize at all. But the words on the side indicated that it was some kind of delivery van. She got out then opened the passenger door to grab her things.

She heard a door open and turned just in time to see a man dressed in black. She saw his face and gasped, recognizing him as the same man from a few weeks ago and from the Station.

"Get in the van, Brighid. You're coming with me."

"No. Who the hell are you?" She stepped away from her car door to close it. He snagged her around the waist. She lost her footing. Her high heel rocked, and she nearly twisted her ankle as he pulled her into the van. She struggled to get free as she kicked and swung her arms. He swung back, backhanding her to the face, splitting her lip, and causing her to fall to the floor of the van. She heard it close hard, and then he was on top of her, hitting her and knocking her in the face, the stomach, and ribs.

"No! Stop it, please. Please," she screamed.

He grabbed her wrists held them together and wrapped some rope around them. She could hardly see through the tears in her eyes and the pain that was making her gasp for breath. Her ribs felt broken, and her cheeks, lips, and eyes throbbed.

He shook her hard, making her head hit the metal of the van. "You stupid bitch. You need to listen to me and obey me. Nothing else exists for you anymore but me. Nothing." He tied her ankles together and then strapped a rope around her waist and secured her to the back of the seat on the passenger side. He climbed over the console and into the driver's seat.

"Here we go, angel of fire. Life is just about to begin for us."

Brighid cried hysterically. She knew who the man was. He had to be the arsonist who'd started all the fires, the killer who murdered people. Why was he taking her? *What could he possibly want with me?*

"Why are you doing this? What is it you want from me?" she cried.

"Your body and your soul."

* * * *

"What the hell do you mean he took her? When? How do you know?" Tobin asked, yelling into the phone at Buddy Landers.

"They found Matt Walsh unconscious in the front seat of the patrol vehicle. He was injected with some sort of chemical that knocked him out. Paramedics are bringing him to the hospital now. Brighid's car door was open and her bags on the ground, plus one high heel. The investigators are here, too. We're looking at the surveillance video, and it looks like the arsonist took her, Tobin. He's driving a black delivery van, and we got an APB out on it now. Jake's getting the helicopters up and sending a message along to the surrounding towns."

"Son of a bitch. I knew I shouldn't have let her go to work alone. She shouldn't even be there."

"I know. The investigators are trying to figure out why he took her. We have the picture of the guy and are spreading it through to all the cops and the public. You should be receiving a text from me now."

Tobin looked at his phone. He pulled over to the side of the road.

"Wait a minute. I've seen this guy before."

"You have? Where?"

"At the Station one night. He started talking to Brighid when she came out of the bathroom, and she looked uncomfortable. I got over to her and was going to introduce myself, but the guy gave me an odd look and then told Brighid he would see her soon. She said she really didn't know him but that he showed up at the office one day and claimed to be a client, but then he left. This is the arsonist? The guy those investigators believe killed those women?"

"Yes."

"Fuck. We have to find her. He'll burn her and then kill her like the others."

"The investigators are looking up any places where he could have taken her in the vicinity. We're also questioning Lenny and Ray. They don't seem to lying about not knowing the arsonist came to take Brighid. They're pretty upset about it."

"I don't believe them. They know something. They have to know a hideout or a safe house for this guy. There's too much money involved to not be prepared. I'm going to get my brothers, and then we're coming there. Someone had to have seen that van."

Tobin turned around and headed back to the house. He called his brother Pat to inform him of the situation and to get ready.

"What the fuck do you mean the arsonist has her? How the hell could this happen? What does he want with her, Tobin?" Pat asked, raising his voice.

"I don't know. I have no fucking clue."

"You said this is the guy they believed murdered women? Burned them in fires? He'll kill Brighid."

"Not if we can figure out where he is and stop him. I need all of you to help me. I'm not going to stand by and wait for the other investigators to try and get a location. The waiting and not physically helping to do something will make me lose my fucking mind. I'm coming by the house now. Get the guys and be ready."

They were going to figure out where this guy had taken Brighid. She had to be scared out of her mind. He'd told her she was safe and that she was protected.

He gripped the steering wheel and felt the tightness in his chest. She was their woman, their responsibility, and he'd failed her. When he thought about having the information about the serial arsonist and about the information the state police investigators gave him about the connection and believing it was the same man, Tobin should have immediately taken precautions, even if they were overkill.

He banged the steering wheel with his fist as he clenched his teeth.

I sat there last night and told her she was safe. I told my brothers that there was nothing to worry about and that this would all be over by tonight.

Brighid could be dead by tonight.

"Fuck, fuck, fuck!"

He thought about his brothers. They were resourceful and well trained. Together, they had to find her. Her life depended upon it.

* * * *

"Holy shit, did you see that?" Billy Parker stated as he swerved his Mustang to the side. A black van came whizzing by him around the corner from his development.

"Billy, what are you doing? Why are you turning around?" Shelly, his girlfriend, asked him as she grabbed onto his arm. He shrugged it free.

"That guy is going to kill someone. There are little kids running around this development waiting for school busses and stuff."

"So we'll call the police and let them handle it. Call your cousin. He's friends with Sheriff McCurran."

Billy shook his head, and as he came around the corner slowly, he saw the van pull into the driveway of an old house, one everyone thought was abandoned. Recently they'd seen lights on inside and knew someone was renting it but never saw a face.

"There, see he lives right there and probably was just in a hurry. Forget about it. I don't want to be late for first period or Mr. Miller is going to give me detention again. It sucks. Come on." She tugged on Billy's sleeve.

He watched the garage door close, and it didn't sit right with him. If he saw that van again driving recklessly, he was definitely going to call his cousin. He turned around and headed back out of the development and right to the high school.

Chapter 8

Brighid could hardly breathe. The air was so thick and she was sweating so much she was passing in and out of consciousness. Sweat dripped from her brow and down her neck, and she wished for something cold, even just a gentle breeze or an open window. She pulled on the bindings. She couldn't see them but felt them against her wrists and against her ankles. She realized, too, that she had no clothes on, only her panties and bra. Everything hurt. Her mouth, her cheeks, her ribs, and her inner thighs. It was pitch-black wherever they were. She inhaled and could smell what she could only describe as a basement odor. Cement, mildew, maybe mothballs. It made her feel sick.

She heard a noise, a scratch-like sound, and then she saw the flame.

She heard his voice.

"You keep fighting me, angel of fire. That's why you pass out. What I gave you this time will make you relax and accept your fate." He brought the candle closer toward her. He turned it sideways and the hot wax dripped onto her skin, singeing her.

"No. No," she cried out, but it sounded as though she was talking so slowly, like some weird cartoon show where the voices were slowed down to sound really weird. He pulled back.

"I have to get you ready. You need to accept my power and to know that I have the ability to control, to create, fire."

She stared at him, her vision not so clear. He had dark hair, big bright gray eyes, and wore no shirt. He had muscles and was lean, but his chest had odd scars on it. They were gashes, lines of burns, and some circular ones, too.

She fisted her hands, and the move made her underarms ache and her elbows scream in protest. What had he done to her while she passed out?

He came closer, holding the candle in one hand then using his other hand to move over her body right above her skin. He didn't touch her, just came so close she shivered and tightened her belly muscles, which caused her to moan and cringe.

"So very beautiful. Your skin is soft, you're muscular, and strong though. You're perfection." He pressed his palm to her belly and applied pressure to her skin. She felt the pain, the achiness, and knew she was bruised, at minimum. His hand moved lower, and his hard palm pressed deeper, making her feel as if he wanted to cause pain to her gut, but then he eased lower and pressed over her mound.

"We're going to be one." He swirled his hand sideways, his fingers grazing her pussy over the panties, and she cried out.

"Don't touch me. Get away from me." The tears streamed down her face, and her head pounded as her eyes lost focus. She definitely wasn't feeling right. He said he'd given her something. He'd drugged her, the prick bastard.

He licked his lips while letting his eyes roam over her breasts. They were barely in the cups of her bra, and she had the feeling he'd touched her as she lay there unconscious. She shivered, her body unable to remain still, as if it remembered the feel of his close proximity and what was to come.

"I'm going to burn you, Brighid. All this practice, this conditioning, is for you so that you can handle the pain of the fire, the flame as it dances upon your skin."

He caressed her skin. His fingers and palm landed on her jaw. He clenched it tight, looked down into her eyes, and licked his lips. "You are so perfect. The others were nothing compared to you. You're the one. I just know it."

He leaned closer, and she tried turning her face away from him, but his grip tightened so hard that she gasped from the pain, the ache in her jaw as his fingers dug in deep. He kissed her. He covered her mouth, plunged his tongue in deeply, and then pulled back and released her jaw as she spit his taste from her mouth. He smacked her. It was swift, hard, and right on point. Her teeth ached, and she cried. But then his hand was on her throat, squeezing, making her see that he had complete power over her like this. She was tied up to the bedposts. She felt the mattress beneath her body. He was going to hurt her, possibly rape her, and there was nothing she could do. She was helpless, and she cried, sobbed until he scraped his nails along her throat and stared down at her skin.

"You see why it's so dark in here? You're going to see when I raise the lights slightly that fire has no shadow. Its light glows from the power within me and the strength I have to defeat all in my path trying to stop me from achieving my goals. I've chosen you to join me."

His nail scraped along her throat to her cleavage. He applied pressure between her breasts and let his finger dip into one cup and then dip into the other. He leaned down, and the candle he held in his hand burned bright, giving off an evil, morbid glow to her surroundings, which would, most likely, become her grave.

She inhaled deeply and felt her stomach concave as he kissed her skin.

"No. I don't want to join you in your darkness. Pick someone else. Leave me alone," she screamed at him.

He slammed his forearm down along her throat, making her gasp and lose her breath. He got up off the bed and flicked on a light, which only slightly illuminated the room. She could see they were in a large basement and that there was a doorway. There didn't seem to be any windows. If there were, then they were covered or hidden. She pulled on her restraints and looked down to see the welts along her skin of her thighs and on her hips and belly. She could see bruising and redness on her ribs. There must be some broken ones. She could hardly take a full breath.

Her head felt fuzzy but not as bad as when she'd first awoken. Could whatever he had given her be wearing off?

She stared at him, the monster that inflicted the pain, as he glided his hand over her skin, right above it, barely touching it. Yet her body reacted. It convulsed and shook with fear of what was to come.

"The perfect canvas for my work." He started breathing a little more rapidly, and it freaked her out. The man was insane. He was a total nut case, and she was going to die here.

He pressed his palm over her skin on her breasts and her belly.

"Perfect, clean, soft, and ready for my touch. No blemishes or scars, no freckles or markings, a pure, clean canvas for me to mark you as my own. Brighid, we're going to be a team. I'm not going to move too fast, no matter how much my need pushes me to that edge. I'm going to take my time, angel." He squeezed her hip and then stared at the flame of the candle and smiled like a screwball.

He reached back for the candle that continued to burn. He moved it over her body and used his other hand to part her skin.

"You need training to prepare you. That's where I went wrong before. The others needed time to adjust to the pain, but I was desperate to achieve my wants and desires. With you, I'll go slow, Brighid. I promise."

He spread her skin on her belly then tipped the candle, making the hot wax land on her belly.

"No. No." She cried out, but he continued to drip the burning-hot wax over her skin.

"Get away from me. I hate you. I hate you, and I won't be yours, ever." She cried out in anger and protest as she pulled on her restraints, causing her wrists and her ankles to burn as the rope cut through her skin. The ache brought the focus off of the hot wax as he continued to move it around her, even over her breasts.

She pooled saliva in her mouth and then spit it at him, stopping him.

"You're not like the others." He shook his head and stood up.

Oh God he's talking about the women he killed.

He gave a soft smile, and then it turned to an angry one. "They weren't like you. They were nothing like you. It just took me this long to figure out exactly what I needed, wanted, to fill that gap, that emptiness I've had since I was a child." He reached out and ran a finger along her jaw, which ached and was surely bruised.

"I want to show you something. Some special reminders of what I went through to get here to you. How I nearly faltered and made some mistakes. I'm sorry, Brighid, but I thought they were perfect, too. But they weren't. Don't be angry or jealous. We're together now, and that's all that matters." He brought over several pictures of different women. Young, pretty women with red hair. He started naming them and talking about who they were and what he had done to them.

She saw the images. The ones when they were perfect, pretty, smiling, and happy. Then he showed the ones where they were bruised. They looked scared but had posed on their knees, hands on their thighs and stared at the camera smiling softly probably because he'd threatened them. He kept showing her more and more, and with each passing photo, the bruises, the fear, the tears, and pain, then blood and burns, attacked her eyes, her mind, and her body. He was going to do the same thing to her. He was going to burn her.

Brighid began to cry. She couldn't help it. She felt so badly for those women. To know they'd suffered such horrible deaths and that she was going to be suffering, too, made her cry harder.

"Shut up. Shut up!" he yelled at her and threw the pictures across the floor. He started tossing things and breaking things in a fit of rage. Then he turned on her and straddled her body. He shook her shoulders and spittle hit her lips and her eyes as she gasped and held her breath, waiting for him to kill her right now this second.

"I am darkness. I am evil, and the fire I have burning within me will be shared with you, and we will be one."

"Oh God no. No, I will not share your evil." She screamed at him, feeling a fight in her and a determination to not cower and lie there in defeat. She would die fighting his attack on her body and what he believed was his ability to take her soul. She was not a religious person, but damn, did she turn to God right now in this moment and beg for the strength to get through this, to fight him in a way that altered this madman's plan to kill her slowly and with fire.

They had to be looking for her. Her men, Tobin, the investigators. It had to be late. Hours must have passed.

"God, help me. Help me, God." She cried out as she pushed upward, trying to get him off of her and show she would fight him till the end.

"Don't bring God into this. He can't help you. He has no power like I do."

He smacked her face, and she screamed for him to stop.

She could tell that he had lost his mind. At any moment he was going to pop and lose it. She knew it.

He eased his body down over hers and began to lick her skin. She shuddered with disgust and hatred for this monster and his sick, delusional mind. Her whole body tightened and convulsed in disgust and horror. She kept screaming and cursing at him until her voice cracked and burned. It felt like sand paper, and she could hardly breathe.

"This body will be mine. I will fill it with darkness and then light it up with the power of the fire within me."

She shook her head. "Like God, I am light. There is no darkness within me, only light, a good, pure, sacred light. You can't ever have me. You won't ever own me," she threatened, not even knowing where the words came from but only feeling the determination to not let him defeat her and break her mind and soul.

He roared as he rose up and slammed his hand down onto her chest. He began to swing at her, striking her in the mouth, the chin and neck, making her cry for mercy. Then he was up and off of her, pacing and running his fingers through his hair. She'd frazzled him, but it had cost her. She was losing her focus again. She begged to remain alert and awake, yet her body yearned for darkness and rest. She was losing this battle. Why wasn't anyone looking for her?

* * * *

"There has to be something, some place, a safe house, a rental somewhere where this guy is staying," Investigator Voigt said. "You're already going to jail for insurance fraud, personal damages to all your victims. If anything happens to Miss Murphy, you'll be a lifer in jail, and that's if her boyfriends don't kill you both first. So start thinking of locations. It's getting dark. He took her over seven hours ago. We want answers. We have all the evidence we need on the computer system, in your hidden files, and that private laptop for real business numbers. Where did this Stark guy take Brighid?"

"I don't know. I swear to you I have no idea. There is no safe house. We didn't even know his name until recently. He's out of control. No one was supposed to get hurt," Lenny yelled back at him.

Trent shoved Lenny back into his chair.

"Let's look over credit card statements and bills. Maybe there was a charge there for something, his monthly bills and expenses?" Investigator Gregory Voight said as Jeffrey started scrolling through the records and everything they had on Lenny and Ray.

Buddy Landers was listening to all of this, and his concern for Brighid grew stronger. His phone started ringing around four thirty. He looked at the caller ID and saw that it was his cousin calling.

"Hey, Ronie, what's up?" he asked as he looked away from Lenny and Ray. He wanted to strangle these guys but was relieved Tobin and his brothers weren't here right now or blood would be shed.

"What did you say? Where? Oh shit, thank that son of yours and be sure to stay clear of the house." Buddy closed up his cell phone.

"I think we just got super fucking lucky. That was Ronie, my cousin, seems his boy was driving into school with his girlfriend this morning and a black van cut him off and made him swerve. He turned around to see where the guy lived and was going to confront him when his girlfriend stopped him. Turned out the guy lives in a rental on the same block. Billy saw the driver put the van in the garage. I've got the address. The kid says it was a black van with the word delivery on it in white. He heard about the APB that was out on the van as he got out of football practice."

"God, I hope this is where this asshole is and that Brighid is okay. Let's head there now. Call Tobin and let him and his brothers know. They're on that side of town now and can move in slowly. We'll be there in ten minutes," Trent Landers said, and Buddy made the call.

* * * *

They were standing outside of the pickup truck. Pat was running his fingers through his hair, feeling like a madman to be out of control like this. For every minute that passed, this psycho serial arsonist-murderer could be inflicting pain on their woman.

"I can't take this. I'm losing my fucking patience. I can't focus. It's been seven fucking hours. Seven," Pat exclaimed.

"I just can't believe this is real. I can't," Reece said and then slammed his hand down on the front hood of the truck.

"I cannot believe that no one saw this black van," Tobin said. "We even have the fucking picture posted on all the main highway information signs throughout town and the emergency broadcast system. By now the majority of citizens in this town should have seen the pictures."

"Maybe he took her out of town immediately? If that's the case, they could be anywhere," Rusty said.

"But someone would have seen them. There's highway and, yes, some remote areas, but it's a distinctive van," Pat said.

"A stolen van from what the investigators gathered. The owner was definitely not connected to this operation," Tobin said.

"Well, you basically shook him until he pissed his pants, so, yes, he's wasn't involved," Reece said, and Pat chuckled.

"Poor guy did nearly piss his pants," Rusty said, and they all got quiet.

Then Tobin's phone rang. They all watched as he answered it.

"What? Holy shit. Okay. Do you seriously want us to wait?"

"What is it? What's going on?" Reece asked.

Tobin disconnected the call. "Get in. We've got a location. Everyone will be there in ten minutes tops."

They got into the truck, and Tobin explained about Buddy and Trent's cousin, some young kid who had called in about seeing the van this morning.

"Why did he wait so long to tell anyone?" Rusty asked.

"The kid was at school then at football practice. Buddy said he heard about the van and the description over the radio, and he called his dad." Tobin gunned it down the highway to the location. Before he made it around the corner, he slowed the truck down and parked it a few houses away.

"What a fucking break. Thank God that kid wasn't some airhead and actually paid attention to what's going on around him," Reece added.

"What's the plan, boss?" Pat asked as they all stared at the house. Pat could hear everyone's low breathing as they just stared at it.

"It's getting fucking dark. We should move before we lose the last bits of light."

"But what if he hears us come in and then hurts her, kills her?" Rusty asked.

"We should check that garage first. Make sure it's the right place," Reece said.

"Let's get out. Reece, Rusty, I want the two of you to come in behind us. Pat and I are law enforcement," Tobin said to his brothers as they all got out of the truck.

"We have our guns, too. We're trained and legally carrying," Reece stated firmly.

Tobin licked his lips and then looked to the right at the other houses.

"Okay, as quiet as possible, let's move in. Reece, Pat, take the back entrance. Rusty and I have the front. We do a sweep of the house and listen for any signs of the location where he's keeping her," Tobin said to them as they checked their weapons.

"In the other cases, he kept them in a dark basement. That's what I read in those reports," Pat said to Tobin. Reece swallowed hard, and Rusty clenched his teeth.

"We do a quick sweep of the first floor and listen. If they are in the basement, we go slowly as to not alert him to our presence. If need be, we charge the basement stairs and get down there as quickly as possible. Got it?" Tobin asked, and they nodded.

"Let's do this. Let's get our woman back," Pat said, and they agreed as they slowly, expertly, like trained men, infiltrated the house.

* * * *

Brighid felt the hands digging into her thighs and her hips. She started to moan and grunt in pain.

"Wake up. It's time for more training," he whispered against her ear and licked the lobe.

She turned her head away from him. "No," she mumbled, her lips so swollen she couldn't talk. Her eyes wouldn't open completely because they were swollen, too.

She lay motionless, and it obviously pissed him off.

"Wake up. Wake the fuck up now." He shoved at her body, and she lay still.

She heard the click of a knife. She saw him standing over her, looking wild and rabid.

"I'll cut you up. I'll hurt you worse if you don't cooperate."

"Screw you, asshole."

She spat at him, and he slashed her skin with the knife right over her rib cage. He came down again and slashed the other side deeper. She screamed at the top of her lungs and then heard a door slam open. She looked up toward the lighted doorway. Like shadows of light in a room of pure evil and darkness, figures appeared. Stark stood up and knocked over his table of items and torturing tools as those shadows descended the stairs. A fire started in the corner when he yelled and threw something at it. Flames emerged, shining the whole room, but he charged with the knife toward the shadows as she screamed.

She heard the multiple gunshots then a large thump. There was yelling and then voices she recognized.

"Jesus, look what he did to you. Oh God, baby, please. I've got you. Please be okay," Rusty said to her. She cried and sobbed uncontrollably.

"There's nothing to put this fire out. We have to move, now," Reece yelled to them.

"He's dead, baby. He can't ever hurt you or anyone else again," Pat said to her as he and Tobin began to slowly cut the bindings on her wrists.

They could hear the sirens blaring in the distance.

"Tobin? You guys in here?" someone else's voice yelled from upstairs.

"Down here. We need a fire extinguisher," Reece yelled up.

Someone caressed her cheek.

"We're going to get you to the hospital, baby. You're going to be okay now. I promise, baby. I'm so sorry this happened. So sorry," Tobin said to her.

She cringed in pain as they undid the bindings and slowly brought her arms down. Others came down the stairs. She could feel so many people down there.

"She's cut on both sides. A knife did the damage there and there," Rusty said, and she blinked her eyes open as she moaned.

"It's Mercury, sweetheart. We're going to get you bandaged up and then onto a stretcher. It's going to be okay."

Someone was caressing her hair from her cheeks and her forehead.

"We're never going to let you out of our sight again. This never should have happened," Tobin whispered, and she felt his lips against her forehead, and she sobbed.

Epilogue

"How is she really?" Buddy asked Tobin when he stopped into the department to sign some papers. He'd taken the next several weeks off to spend with Brighid and his brothers. They needed the time together. They needed to process what had happened, to help her heal and feel safe, and work on their plans for the future.

Tobin sat forward in the chair in front of Jake's desk. Buddy, and Trent were there, too. .

"She has nightmares, needs to take some medication for that. The stitches come out tomorrow, and we have an appointment with a great plastic surgeon that Kyle St. James recommended. I think if we can get those marks from the knife wounds to disappear then she may be able to mentally heal better."

"How about the other bruises and welts? All gone?" Trent asked.

"Still visible but her ribs are wrapped up so the bandages hide them. It's fucking crazy. I just want to take all her pain away."

"That's understandable, and it will take time. I heard that she started seeing that therapist Michaela and Serefina recommended. That will help a bunch too," Jake said to him.

"It will. This whole community has been amazing and supportive. People keep dropping things off and offering assistance. Thank God that cousin of yours saw that van that day, Trent, Buddy. I don't even want think about if he hadn't," Tobin said, and Buddy smiled.

"Billy is a good kid. A bit of a wiseass now and then, but he's very alert and in tune to his surroundings. He wants to be a cop someday too," Trent stated.

"Well, he might just make a really good one. I'd better get moving. I want to pick up some stuff for lunch and head home. Thanks for everything." He shook their hands.

"Take your time, Tobin. There's no rush to get back here. You've got a lot of vacation time saved," Jake said as they all walked him out.

"Don't worry, I will. My brothers and I need to work out a schedule. None of us will be leaving her alone for quite some time."

They smiled and nodded in understanding, and Tobin headed out to get home.

Things had changed so much. The safe and secure feeling he'd always had in Treasure Town had been tainted by some madman who wanted to cause havoc and pain. He needed to make Brighid and his brothers feel safe again. He needed to hold her in his arms and know she was protected. He hurried up to get home.

* * * *

Brighid knew they were surprised that she wanted to take a walk by the beach. She had been inside for more than a week now, and she hated it. She wanted to start living and putting the traumatic event behind her.

She closed her eyes as Rusty helped her get dressed. She made it simple by putting on a sundress that slid right over her head. His lips kissed every bit of skin they could as he assisted her. Her men were so empathetic and caring. They took every opportunity to hold her, kiss her, and make love to her slowly. Her ribs were still sore, and the stitches still needed to be removed, so making love was difficult, but they took their time and loved her one by one.

"Are you ready?" Rusty asked her, holding her by her hips as he stared down into her eyes.

"In just a minute. You go downstairs, and I'll meet you."

He squinted at her. They had never left her side. Not since that day she was abducted and tortured and they had saved her.

He slowly left her, but his eyes, his body language, indicated that he wasn't happy about it.

He left the room, and she looked into the mirror as she brushed her hair.

The bruising was faint but still noticeable.

She took a deep breath and felt the emptiness of the room, that anxious feeling instant because her men weren't by her side. She needed them so much her heart ached to not have them right there with her.

She took a deep breath and walked down the stairs. As the sun cast light through the room where they all stood waiting for her, she paused in awe.

Just as that day when she'd felt there was no help and she would die there in the darkness at the hands of a serial arsonist, her body aching, her heart, her will to live being tested to the very last ounce of determination, she saw them. Her shadows of light at the top of the stairs ready to come to her aid and rescue. They were her lovers, her best friends, her everything. They were what kept her fighting, her needing, wanting to survive so she could be with them.

The tears stung her eyes, and instantly Tobin was there, pulling her into his arms from the last two steps of the staircase. She wrapped her arms around him, and he held her close as he brought her to the others. They gathered around her, touched her, caressed her body and laid kisses to her shoulders, her head, and her arms, infusing their love, their healing capabilities into her, and she loved them for it.

She pulled back to look down into Tobin's eyes.

"Are you okay?" he asked.

"I just love you all so much. I need you so much. Even being away from you for a minute makes me feel anxious and nervous."

"We won't ever leave you, baby. We'll always be right nearby." Rusty kissed the top of her hand. She chuckled.

"I don't want to be clingy. It won't always have to be this way. Where I'll need to feel your hands on me, holding me, touching me.

Feel your lips against my skin and smell your cologne. Let your scent fill my nostrils and make me feel safe and complete."

"Why the hell not? We need the same things from you. To feel you close, to take from this body and give of ours to you," Pat said to her.

"To smell the scent of your shampoo and your perfume that lingers in a room after you've been there," Rusty said.

"To smell the pillow on the bed and know you're right next to me when I awake in the night with fear or uncertainty that you're really ours," Tobin told her.

"We love you so much, baby. It's going to take time to get through this, but we will, and one day, it will be but a distant memory. You fought so hard, and you're a survivor. Survivors live on. They never quit, they never give up or give in. They triumph, and we'll be here to witness it every day for the rest of our lives," Reece told her and kissed her arm.

She felt the tears roll down her cheeks, and Tobin wiped them away and smiled.

"How about we pack up some sandwiches and turn this little beach trip into a picnic?" he suggested.

She smiled wide and felt the excitement, the encouragement to do something so damn normal.

"Yes." She kissed him, and then he set her feet down on the floor, and they all worked together to make sandwiches, pack up a cooler, and grab all the things they would need for a nice picnic on the beach.

She absorbed the moment. Stashed it away as a happy, carefree time when she realized, once again, that her four first responders set her heart on fire. No matter what life might bring them, even in the darkest of times, she could count on her four sexy first responders to be her shadows of light, her strength to go one and to prevail, no matter what obstacles lay ahead. She smiled wide and then gasped as Pat wrapped his arms around her from behind and kissed her neck. He inhaled against her skin, and she held on tightly, loving it, loving him, and looking forward to making love together to end the day perfectly.

THE END

WWW.DIXIELYNNDWYER.COM

ABOUT THE AUTHOR

People seem to be more interested in my name than where I get my ideas for my stories from. So I might as well share the story behind my name with all my readers.

My momma was born and raised in New Orleans. At the age of twenty, she met and fell in love with an Irishman named Patrick Riley Dwyer. Needless to say, the family was a bit taken aback by this as they hoped she would marry a family friend. It was a modern day arranged marriage kind of thing and my momma downright refused.

Being that my momma's families were descendents of the original English speaking Southerners, they wanted the family blood line to stay pure. They were wealthy and my father's family was poor.

Despite attempts by my grandpapa to make Patrick leave and destroy the love between them, my parents married. They recently celebrated their sixtieth wedding anniversary.

I am one of six children born to Patrick and Lynn Dwyer. I am a combination of both Irish and a true Southern belle. With a name like Dixie Lynn Dwyer it's no wonder why people are curious about my name.

Just as my parents had a love story of their own, I grew up intrigued by the lifestyles of others. My imagination as well as my need to stray from the straight and narrow made me into the woman I am today.

For all titles by Dixie Lynn Dwyer, please visit
www.bookstrand.com/dixie-lynn-dwyer

Siren Publishing, Inc.
www.SirenPublishing.com

Lightning Source UK Ltd.
Milton Keynes UK
UKHW02f2224271117
313459UK00008B/1359/P